IT'S
MURDER
WITH DOVER

**Books by Phoebe Atwood Taylor
available from Foul Play Press**

Asey Mayo Cape Cod Mysteries

THE ANNULET OF GILT
THE ASEY MAYO TRIO
BANBURY BOG
THE CAPE COD MYSTERY
THE CRIMINAL C.O.D.
THE CRIMSON PATCH
THE DEADLY SUNSHADE
DEATH LIGHTS A CANDLE
DIPLOMATIC CORPSE
FIGURE AWAY
GOING, GOING, GONE
THE MYSTERY OF THE CAPE COD PLAYERS
THE MYSTERY OF THE CAPE COD TAVERN
OCTAGON HOUSE
OUT OF ORDER
THE PERENNIAL BOARDER
PROOF OF THE PUDDING
PUNCH WITH CARE
SANDBAR SINISTER
SPRING HARROWING
THE SIX IRON SPIDERS
THREE PLOTS FOR ASEY MAYO

Writing as Alice Tilton

BEGINNING WITH A BASH
FILE FOR RECORD
HOLLOW CHEST
THE LEFT LEG

IT'S MURDER WITH DOVER

Joyce Porter

A Foul Play Press Book

The Countryman Press, Inc.
Woodstock, Vermont

Copyright © 1973 By Joyce Porter

This edition first published in 1992 by Foul Play Press, an
imprint of The Countryman Press, Inc., Woodstock, VT 05091

ISBN 0-88150-233-2

Printed in the United States of America

10 9 8 7 6 5 4 3 2 1

IT'S
MURDER
WITH DOVER

One

'It might perhaps be an idea to call Scotland Yard in?'

On the other side of the exquisite Early Empire desk the Chief Constable winced. Talk about an iron command in a velvet question! 'Oh, do you think so?' he asked, failing to keep the resentment out of his voice.

Lord Crouch did think so but, being a man of few words and enormous influence, he didn't have to keep saying so. He smiled a deprecatory smile.

The Chief Constable got his handkerchief out and blew his nose. 'My chaps could cope perfectly well, you know,' he muttered. 'They'd be very discreet, too.'

'I am not asking for any preferential treatment,' said Lord Crouch in a tone which almost took the sting out of the rebuke.

Not bloody much! thought the Chief Constable. He stuffed his handkerchief back in his pocket and tried to work out what His Nibs was up to this time. Why on earth did he want Scotland Yard brought in to deal with a murder which, whatever else it was, was certainly a purely local affair?

From outside the door came another sequence of those muted sounds which punctuated life at Beltour. First there was the rather hesitant trampling of many feet. Then a lot of shuffling. When this died down, a solo voice could be heard, rattling monotonously through its recitation.

Lord Crouch took no notice but the Chief Constable's eyes flickered as light dawned. So that was it! He glanced at Lord Crouch with grudging admiration. Well, you had to hand it to him! Where the promotion of his ancestral home was concerned, he never missed a trick.

The Chief Constable ventured a sly dig. 'There'll be a lot more publicity if we call the Yard in.'

If this observation had scored a palpable hit, Lord Crouch didn't show it. He merely raised his eyebrows, as he did everything else, very, very slowly. 'We all have our crosses to bear, Mr Pinkham.'

You old devil! thought the Chief Constable. Some village lad gets himself battered to death in the grounds of Beltour and all his flipping lordship can think about is how to cash in on it! Free publicity? He'd sell his grandmother for it! Give him half a chance and he'd blow up this routine rural slaying into the crime of the century. Oh, Mr Pinkham could see it all now! The newspaper headlines, Lord Crouch's long face on every television screen in the country, and another 5p on top of your entrance fee to view the murder spot. It would make a nice additional attraction for the kids who'd already seen the boa constrictors and the miniature Chinese torture chamber.

The Chief Constable made his final effort. 'We can ask for help from the Yard, of course,' he allowed gloomily, 'but that doesn't say we'll get it. They may well think that this is a case we should handle ourselves.'

You didn't put a spoke in Lord Crouch's wheel that easily. 'Just mention my name to the Commissioner,' he murmured.

The Chief Constable stood up. He should have taken a stronger line, he knew that. Told old Crouch to stuff it. Pointed out that, far from him sitting there calling the tune, he should by rights be down in the Interview Room at the nick answering a few searching questions about his own role in the drama. The Chief Constable sighed. He should never have come cap-in-hand to Beltour in the first place. Wouldn't have done if it hadn't been for Mrs Pinkham and her social ambitions. She'd never let him hear the last of it if he didn't keep in with Lord Crouch. Ah, me – the lengths some women would go to for the sake of that invitation to the Annual Sherry and Cheese Biscuit Party!

'Well, I suppose I'd better go and get on with it,' he said. 'No,' – as a thin, bony hand began to move towards the bell push – 'there's no need to disturb anybody, my lord. I can see myself out.'

Lord Crouch remained seated behind his magnificent desk. It wasn't that he wished to be discourteous to Mr Pinkham; it was merely that, at six foot seven in his socks, he didn't care much for standing in close proximity to anybody. It made, he felt, both parties look ridiculous. His little foible was well known throughout the county and the Chief Constable, touchy as he was about the respect due to his office, didn't give it a second thought.

Lord Crouch let his visitor get right to the door before firing his final shot, if that isn't too violent an expression for the gentle statement which wafted down the entire length of the Malplaquet Library. 'The Scotland Yard detective will, of course, stay here at Beltour as my guest.'

That brought the Chief Constable up with a jerk and, not being too skilled in the art of conversation down the length of a cricket pitch, he came back a few yards. 'Here in the house, sir? Well, I don't know that they'll be too keen on that. I'll ask 'em, of course, but . . .' His voice trailed away, lost in the famous vaulted ceiling and the decidedly cool silence in which his objections were being received. He tried again. 'There's likely to be two of them, sir.'

'Oh?'

'There'll be an assistant, sir. A sergeant.'

3

Lord Crouch had no intention of extending his hospitality to cover the entire Metropolitan Police Force. 'He can stay in the village. At The Bull Reborn. You'll see to that, will you?'

'Certainly, my Lord,' said the Chief Constable miserably, and withdrew in poor order.

Now, the trouble with pulling strings is that one can never be absolutely sure what is on the other end and Lord Crouch's experience may serve as a warning to all those who are tempted to manipulate the system for their own ignoble purposes. The old-boy network can, on occasion, trawl up some very queer fish.

Not that Lord Crouch's name was really cutting much ice by the time the request for assistance in the Beltour murder descended on the right desk in Scotland Yard. The Commander in charge of the Murder Squad had heard of Beltour, of course. He'd taken his kids there for the day a couple of years ago and reckoned he'd been swindled.

'Why can't these country bumpkins do their own dirty work?' he demanded, tossing the very high level memo across to his secretary. 'Well, I can't spare anybody. We're stretched to the limit as it is.'

The secretary slid the memo back in front of his master and tempted him. 'Detective Chief Inspector Dover is due back from sick leave tomorrow, sir.'

'Dover? I'd forgotten about him – thank God!' An evil grin spread over the Commander's face. 'Do you think we dare?'

'I don't see that he can object to being recalled a few hours early, sir. After all, he fiddles more time off with that disgusting stomach of his than the rest of the squad put together.'

'Good God!' exploded the Commander. 'I'm not worried about Dover's bloody feelings! If he doesn't like it, he can do the other – and welcome. No, it's this Lord Crouch I'm wondering about. I mean, how big a stink is he capable of kicking up?'

'Oh, not much,' said the secretary, already reaching for the telephone. 'What's a peer of the realm these days? Besides, he's the one who's asked for our help, isn't he? He ought to be grateful he's getting anybody.'

'True,' agreed the Commander doubtfully as his secretary picked up the receiver. 'But Dover's not a proper member of the Murder Squad, you know. I mean, we've only been lumbered with the fat old layabout because nobody else'll have him, not even as a holiday relief. I should have threatened to hand in my resignation like everybody else did,' he added sorrowfully. 'I would have done, too, if I'd known what I was in for.'

The secretary, who was twice as decisive as the Commander could ever hope to be, began to dial. 'Chief Inspector Dover is attached to the Murder Squad as a supernumerary,' he pointed out. 'No civilian's ever going to know the difference.'

'I don't know why you think that makes it any better,' grumbled the Commander. 'I mean, suppose they think we're all like him?'

The secretary stayed his finger. At times one couldn't help wishing for a little more backbone. 'Well, what do you want me to do, sir?' he asked. 'Ship Dover off into the wilds or have him hanging around here making the place look untidy?'

Faced with a Hobson's choice like that, even the Commander managed to make up his mind and his secretary finished dialling Dover's number. When it was ringing out he offered the receiver to the Commander. 'Do you want to break the glad tidings to him, sir, or shall I?'

As the Commander suddenly remembered an urgent engagement elsewhere, Detective Chief Inspector Dover was obliged to hear the painful news that he was expected to do some work for his money from the mouth of a mere underling.

Not that Dover submitted to either indignity without protest. For a man supposedly still on his sick bed, he displayed a remarkable vigour – arguing, whining, cajoling and threatening. It was all to no avail. The secretary blandly insisted that he was just a messenger boy, powerless to alter the instructions, and that the Commander was simply not available and wouldn't rescind his orders if he were.

Dover cursed the Commander's forebears back to the fourth and fifth generation and then made the fatal mistake of pausing for breath before starting on the secretary's equally suspect ancestry.

The secretary seized his chance. 'Well, I'm sorry, sir,' he said with cheerful callousness, 'but you know how it is. When you've gotta go, you've gotta go! The best of luck!' He hung up.

By the time, early the following morning, Dover had been loaded on to the train which was to take him as near to his destination as British Rail could manage these days, he had got his second wind and a new audience. His assistant, whipping boy and general dog's-body – Detective Sergeant MacGregor – sat and suffered on the opposite seat in the compartment. Young, elegant and fed-up to the back teeth, he had heard all Dover's grievances many times before and he found them just as boring on this occasion as he had done in the past. Long before the dreary London suburbs had been left behind, MacGregor found his mind wandering to pleasanter pastures. Take reincarnation, now! That was an interesting idea. There was probably something in it, too. MacGregor glanced at the scruffy, bowler-hatted hulk grizzling away in its corner and suppressed a deep sigh of self pity. What other explanation except reincarnation could there be for the unholy alliance into which he had been forced with Dover? Only some vile and unspeakable wickedness in an earlier existence could possibly have earned such

6

a fearful punishment in this one.

The journey took two hours but Dover was still going great guns as he reluctantly deposited his unwieldy seventeen and a quarter stone on the station platform. It was raining heavily and, while he stood waiting impatiently for Sergeant MacGregor to struggle out with the baggage, steady trickles of water began dripping off the brim of his bowler onto his overcoat. Within seconds the generous sprinkling of dandruff on the shoulders had been churned into an unsavoury, muddy slime. Dover scowled bleakly and looked round for a new victim on whom to vent his spite. One came, all unknowing, speeding down the platform towards him.

Now that the calling in of Scotland Yard was *fait accompli*, Mr Pinkham, the Chief Constable, had determined to make the best of it. It was no good crying over spilt milk and they were all working towards the same end, weren't they? Heaven only knew, the local police force was bedevilled enough with internecine vendettas of its own without adding a major feud with Scotland Yard to their number. No, Mr Pinkham's mind was quite made up: total cooperation and all shoulders to the wheel! That way they'd see the back of these stuck-up, interfering bastards from London all the quicker.

Mr Pinkham splashed to a halt, composed his face into a frank and sincerely welcoming smile, and held out his hand.

Dover glared at the proffered limb with undisguised loathing. 'I've been dragged from a bed of suffering to come here!' he snarled.

The Chief Constable's mouth flapped like a newly washed shirt in a stiff breeze. God knows, he'd not expected to be embraced warmly on both cheeks but this was.... 'Are you Detective Chief Inspector Dover?' he spluttered.

'No!' sneered Dover, turning away to head for the station exit and, hopefully, somewhere to sit down. 'I'm little bloody Lord Fauntleroy!'

This unceremonious departure left Mr Pinkham and MacGregor to amuse each other.

'He's not been feeling very well lately,' explained Mac-Gregor, somewhat inadequately.

'Oh,' said the Chief Constable.

'Er – should we perhaps move out of the rain, sir? There's no point in standing here and getting drenched, is there?'

'No,' said the Chief Constable, though his mind was on other things. He made an effort and pulled himself together. 'Well, come on then!' he said.

Dover was already ensconced in the waiting police car, occupying without effort the whole of the back seat. After a moment's hesitation Mr Pinkham got in front with the driver and left MacGregor to squeeze as best he could into one of the tip-up seats.

Now that he'd got the weight off his poor old feet again, Dover was in a better humour. 'Does it always rain like this in this crummy dump?' he asked.

Mr Pinkham's sharp intake of breath was clearly audible but, with his police driver a highly intrigued witness, he hardly felt he could start giving back as good as he got. He sought for the soft answer and forced it out through clenched teeth. 'No,' he said.

Dover examined the passing scenery and pronounced his considered verdict. ' 'Strewth, what a lousy hole!'

'Ah, but I think you'll be pretty impressed when you see Beltour,' said the Chief Constable, all but rupturing himself in the effort to speak calmly.

'Beltour?' demanded Dover. 'What's Beltour when it's at home?'

Mr Pinkham was beginning to feel that he'd strayed into a nightmare. 'Beltour's the place where the murder happened.'

'Oh, *that*!' Dover's interest in the conversation evaporated and with a grunt he burrowed back even deeper into the folds of his overcoat. 'Wake me when we get there!'

For the next quarter of an hour nobody spoke. There was, after all, nothing much to say and the snorts, groans and snores coming from the back seat would have made any exchange of small talk rather difficult. In the end, however, Mr Pinkham was obliged to break the impasse. He turned round gingerly in his seat and addressed himself to MacGregor.

'What will he want to do first, do you think?' he whispered. 'Visit our murder headquarters or get himself settled in?'

MacGregor knew the answer to that one, all right.

The Chief Constable sighed and nodded to his driver. 'You'd better go straight to Beltour House, then.'

MacGregor raised his eyebrows. 'Beltour House, sir?'

'Lord Crouch has very kindly offered your chief inspector accommodation there. Unfortunately there isn't room for you as well so we've booked you in at the village pub.'

MacGregor closed the file in which he had been trying to mug up on the case. 'I'm afraid that's quite out of the question, sir!'

They were speaking as softly as they could but Dover, never one to be caught napping where his personal comfort was concerned, was already cocking an attentive ear.

'Well, I'm not saying that The Bull Reborn is exactly a five star establishment, sergeant, but I'm sure you'll be quite. . .'

MacGregor shook his head impatiently and tapped the file on his knees. 'According to your own initial investigations, sir, Lord Crouch could be personally involved in this case. Chief Inspector Dover cannot possibly compromise his position by accepting his Lordship's hospitality.'

'Ho, can't he?'

Dover, wide awake, was heaving himself upright on the back seat and gawping in pop-eyed wonder through the streaming windows. The car had just swung off the main

9

road into the two-mile drive which swept up to Beltour and the house itself was now coming into view.

' 'Strewth!' gasped Dover with that native vulgarity which never failed to make MacGregor cringe. 'Get a load of that! Blimey, it must be bigger than Buckingham Palace!'

'Not only bigger,' put in the Chief Constable with touching local chauvinism, 'but better, too. In every way. Beltour is one of the finest gems of our national heritage.'

Dover smacked his lips.

MacGregor went on trying to avert disaster. 'I was just explaining to Mr Pinkham, sir, that you can't possibly be Lord Crouch's guest because. . . .'

Dover dragged his greedy little eyes away from the glories of Beltour and directed them on his sergeant. 'Why don't you belt up?' he demanded furiously. 'I reckon it's very kind of Lord Who's-your-father and it'll be nice and handy being right on the spot. Me,' – he jerked a greasy thumb – 'I'm staying there!'

Two

If Lord Crouch got considerably more than he bargained for, Detective Chief Inspector Dover soon found that he had got considerably less.

At first everything in the garden was lovely and Dover tackled the huge flight of granite steps up to Beltour's massive front doors with hardly a complaint and no more than his usual shortness of breath. MacGregor, boot-faced and still sulking, tugged at the wrought-iron bell pull and prepared to greet Lord Crouch when that nobleman came to open the door. MacGregor, the product of a very minor public school, was not to be fooled by this outward display of opulence. He knew all about the plight of the aristocracy in these egalitarian days and he was deeply sympathetic. His heart bled for any man who was forced to have the hoi-polloi trampling through his home at 25p a nob. And those old family retainers! All gone now and replaced by a couple of shifty-eyes foreigners who only served you for the money. MacGregor made up his mind to be very nice indeed to poor Lord Crouch.

'Well?'

MacGregor came out of a delightful reverie in which he

and Lord Crouch were getting on together like a house on fire to find himself being scrutinized in a most patronizing manner not by a belted earl but by a butler. And a very imposing butler, too. MacGregor had never actually encountered a real-life butler before and it quite put him off his stride. He stammered out a very forlorn little account of who they were as Mr Pinkham, his good resolutions already fading, had somewhat discourteously remained in the car.

The butler, from the top of his bald head to the soles of his flat feet, was clearly not pleased. 'Policemen? You're supposed to use the back door, you are. Anyhow,' – he relented against his better judgement – 'you'd better come in now you're here. His Lordship is expecting you.'

It was Dover who rose to the dignity of the occasion. 'Lead on, my man!' he trumpeted with great panache and surged forward to take possession of what he had already come to think of as his own. MacGregor slunk after him.

It has been opined that you could drill a regiment (guards', of course) in the entrance hall at Beltour. This is no doubt an exaggeration but it was certainly a very large place and quite dwarfed the souvenir stall and picture-postcard stand which were, apart from a suit of rusty armour and a couple of showcases, its only furnishings. Through an archway on the right the next convoy of paying customers could be seen, forming up in an untidy crocodile as they waited for their guide. They were admitted to the house only by a side entrance and were temporarily forbidden access to the hall by a rope barrier. Nobody could stop them looking, though, and they pressed forward eagerly as the little procession made its way across the wide open spaces. 'That'll be the cops!' they told each other knowledgeably and fathers hoisted their sons on high so as not to miss the only free show that was likely to fall to their lot on that particular outing.

It was a long trek and both Dover and the butler were showing signs of strain long before they were within sight of the door of the Malplaquet Library. Their laborious progress gave MacGregor plenty of time to display an intelligent interest in his surroundings. He bestowed a knowing nod on the suit of armour before turning a shrewd, connoisseur's eye on the family coronation robes in the first showcase. The second showcase rated a faintly amused smile. It contained, according to the carefully printed notice, the actual garments worn by the present Lord Crouch when performing his National Service with the Royal South Shires Fusiliers (Princess Mabel's Own). The khaki battle dress with its single modest pip on each shoulder and the crumpled beret with the hairy, pale pink hackle may have been short on glamour but they were very strong on human appeal. Even the nobility, they hinted, had done their bit.

The butler opened the library door and Dover all but blotted his copy-book as he realized that his marathon march was still not over. However, he strangled the oaths in time and, gritting his National Health teeth, limped off towards the distant prospect of Lord Crouch.

The social preliminaries were soon dispensed with and MacGregor, to his chagrin, found himself being dismissed to get on with his own mundane affairs. The butler withdrew at the same time, creaking gingerly back down the length of the library.

Lord Crouch moved reluctantly out from behind the sanctuary of his desk. 'Well, we'll move upstairs now, shall we, Mr Dover? Lunch should be just about ready.'

Dover appreciated a man who got his priorities right.

'I'll go first, if you don't mind.'

'Age before beauty!' responded Dover, so much on his best behaviour that it was almost beginning to hurt. He was about to follow Lord Crouch when an antique silver ink-stand on the desk caught his eye. 'Strewth, he'd wager that was worth a pretty penny! You could tell by the size of the thing. Not that it wasn't still highly portable. You could slip it under your coat as easy as. . . .

Dover was saved from further temptation as he realized that Lord Crouch's loping stride had already carried him three quarters of the way down the room. Another minute and he'd be over the flipping horizon.

It was a lead which Dover never managed to pin back as they progressed from room to room, through endless corridors and galleries, across spacious halls and, once, right round three sides of an enormous music room. From time to time they encountered flagging groups of visitors and easily distracted their attention from the Adam fireplaces and those inevitable Italian ceilings. When they finally reached a precipitous flight of stairs, the chief inspector gave up even trying to catch his host up.

'My sister and I have our private apartments at the top of the Acquitaine Tower,' explained Lord Crouch, pausing to peer down over the banisters in an effort to see where this peculiar policeman had got to. 'It's rather a climb but the view makes it well worth while.'

A couple of flights below and with the blood pounding in his ears, Dover most sincerely doubted it but he was in no condition to argue. He barely had the strength to wonder if he wasn't going to pay too high a price for the goodies to come.

As Lord Crouch reached the top landing his sister, Lady Priscilla, came out to join him. Together they listened to the distressing gulping and panting coming up the well of the staircase.

'Nearly there now,' said Lord Crouch, gently encouraging.

'We really ought to install a lift,' murmured Lady Priscilla and nervously asked herself if the man's face was usually such a peculiar colour.

Dover made it and sagged to his knees only when he was sure that blue-blooded hands were outstretched to sustain him. Lord Crouch and Lady Priscilla hoisted him up the last step or two and between them manhandled him into the drawing-room. Dover collapsed into a chair, flopped back with his eyes closed and got down to brass tacks.

'Brandy!' he gasped. 'Or whisky!'

But Lady Priscilla, twenty years a Girl Guide captain, president of the local Red Cross and founder-patron of the Friends of the Edwina, Dowager Lady Crouch Cottage Hospital knew better than to administer alcohol as a restorative. She fancied she knew a more efficacious stimulant and, in due course, she administered it.

The shock of undiluted cold water would have brought Dover back from the dead.

'You see!' beamed Lady Priscilla triumphantly, catching the glass just before it hit the floor. 'I thought that would perk you up all right! Now, do you want to go to your room first and wash your hands or have lunch?'

'Have lunch!' said Dover who was a noted trencherman and thought too much washing weakened you.

Lady Priscilla led the way into the dining-room.

'It's not,' she explained a little later as she ladled out a generous teaspoonful of spinach soup, 'that we are at all fanatical about vegetarianism. We just happen to prefer it. Now, come along, Boys, dear,' – she addressed her brother across a fine Victorian mahogany dining table which had surely seen better days – 'pour the chief inspector out a glass of turnip juice!'

Dover cleared a dry throat. 'Bread?' he asked.

Lady Priscilla's off-hand regrets augured ill for the future. 'It's almost as bad for you as potatoes,' she said and returned to sipping her soup with a thoughtful air. 'Hm, I really think this new recipe I found in the Church Magazine has turned out quite well, don't you, Boys?'

And Dover, who in spite of much evidence to the contrary really was a trained detective, felt his heart and stomach sink even further. Lady Priscilla must do her own cooking! The blows were falling thick and fast.

With the sort of rations that were being served (a goat's

cheese salad followed the soup), there was ample time for conversation. It was Lady Priscilla who willingly shouldered the burden of amusing their distinguished guest and she naturally selected the topic which might be supposed to be uppermost in his mind. It is hardly her fault if she was wrong.

'Mind you,' she began, swallowing down a mouthful of boiled nettles, 'it's poor Miss Marsh that I feel sorry for. She's Gary Marsh's aunt, you know, Mr Dover. She's brought him up ever since he was a tiny baby.'

Dover was staring sadly at his empty plate. 'Gary Marsh?' he echoed dully.

Lady Priscilla blinked. 'The young man who was battered to death near the Donkey Bridge on Sunday night.'

Dover could think of worse ways to go.

'We knew him quite well, didn't we, Boys? Of course one knows everybody in a small community like ours but Miss Marsh has worked for us here at Beltour for over a quarter of a century so we've naturally always taken a keen interest in her affairs. Oh, poor Gary! I remember him coming here as though it was yesterday. Such a sweet little mite, he was! But, then,' – she sighed deeply – 'people always say that about them, don't they?'

It is improbable that Lady Priscilla had ever had anybody belch out loud at her luncheon table before and she innocently interpreted Dover's effort as a question.

'Love children, chief inspector! Didn't you know that Gary Marsh was an illegitimate child? Oh, his aunt's never made any bones about it. Well, country people don't bother much about that sort of thing. They never did. No, it wasn't the fact that he was born out of wedlock that caused the talk. It was who his mother was that had all the tongues wagging.'

Lord Crouch paused with a dried prune halfway to his mouth and glanced across at his sister with a slight frown. 'Now, Prissy, I'm sure Mr Dover doesn't want to hear all this old village gossip.'

'Of course he does, Boys!' retorted Lady Priscilla cheerfully. 'It's background material. And I don't know what you're getting into such a tizzy about because, if I don't tell him, somebody else will.' She gave Dover a conspiratorial grin. 'You do want me to go on, don't you?'

All Dover's interest was currently centred on the pangs of hunger that were gnawing at his vitals but Lady Priscilla had already classified him as one of those horny-handed sons of the soil from whom a certain amount of taciturnity was only to be expected.

'Yes,' she went on, 'well, I'm afraid nobody really believed this story about Miss Marsh's sister and it's quite true that her name had never so much as been mentioned in Beltour until little Gary appeared on the scene. Mind you, Miss Marsh has always been one for keeping herself very much to herself, and being a "foreigner" didn't help. The locals used to be very suspicious of "foreigners".'

'Still are,' said Lord Crouch, placing his knife and fork tidily together on his plate.

'Everybody finished?' Lady Priscilla began collecting up the empty dishes. 'Did I tell you that Miss Marsh first came here as my personal maid when I was just a slip of a girl, Mr Dover? My goodness, that dates me, doesn't it? Well, I'm afraid I can't help that. She was my maid and a very good one, too. I used to call her Milly then, of course. Oh, I remember how terribly upset I was when I had to let her go after dear Papa died! Still, it all worked out very well in the end.'

Lord Crouch had been watching Dover from beneath lowered lids. 'You're rambling again, Prissy!' he warned.

'Am I, dear?' Lady Priscilla loped off quite unperturbed to the kitchen and returned with a small bowl of jelly and an even smaller bowl of cream. 'Well, I'm sure Mr Dover will stop me if there's anything he doesn't understand.' She disappeared into the kitchen again, having forgotten the plates.

Dover, who after all at some stage in the proceedings had certainly been urged to make himself at home, now did so. He dragged the bowl of jelly in front of him and morosely tipped the entire contents of the cream dish over it. By the time Lady Priscilla came back with the pudding plates he had wolfed the lot and was already wiping his mouth with the back of his hand.

This is where breeding tells. Lady Priscilla didn't so much as glance at her brother but set the plates down quietly on the table and resumed her seat. 'Yes,' she said, 'everything seemed to happen at once, the year dear Papa died. He'd been very – well – difficult towards the end and I was really quite worn out with nursing him. He wouldn't allow anybody else near him, you see. Boys was away in the army in those days and that meant there wasn't much he could do to help. Well, when Papa finally died, everybody said I simply must get away for a long holiday. I wanted to, of course, but there was the problem of Beltour. The house wasn't open to the public at that time but that didn't mean you could just walk away and leave it. Boys tried to resign his commission but the authorities wouldn't let him. It was quite ridiculous. I mean, to hear them talk, you'd have thought the safety of the country depended on him. Well, I'd more or less resigned myself to holding the fort and struggling on as best I could until Boys finished his National Service when I got this letter from Cousin Eleanora in America, inviting me to go on this cruise round the world with her. All expenses paid. Eleanora is a cousin on my mother's side, you know, and she married very well. Her husband. . .'

Lord Crouch was now staring at Dover quite openly. He was an odd sort of fish, and no mistake. Not a bit like Lord Crouch had expected. Look at the fellow now, for goodness sake! Slumped down in his chair, eyes closed, mouth open and his chins falling down on his chest like a concertina. Taking it all in, of course. Lord Crouch had no doubts about that. There'd be a razor sharp brain ticking away like mad behind that fat and pasty face. Still, – Lord Crouch slowly uncoiled a yard or two of leg which had got twisted round his chair – maybe the poor chap was getting the smallest touch bored. Once she'd got the bit between her teeth, Prissy did tend to run on.

Lord Crouch tried to speed things up. 'We decided to close Beltour completely for a year,' he said, interrupting his sister just when she was getting to the Texan oil wells. 'That meant dismissing most of the staff, of course. Some of them we lost for good but a few of them took unpaid leave of absence for a year and came back to us when we re-opened the house. Miss Marsh belonged to the latter category.'

The change of voice certainly roused Dover and he glowered resentfully for a few moments at Lord Crouch. Then his grasshopper brain latched on to a new distraction and he fell to sucking his teeth in the desperate hope that some particle of food might have got trapped behind his dentures.

It took more than a fraternal intervention to shut Lady Priscilla up. 'Yes, that's right,' she agreed. 'Miss Marsh went up north somewhere to stay with her parents and she took a temporary job while I was away on my wonderful cruise with Cousin Eleanora. Then we were all united again when Boys came out of the army. My goodness, that was the beginning of some hard work, wasn't it, Boys? You see, Mr Dover, my brother decided that the only way to make ends meet was to turn Beltour into one of these stately homes and open it to the public. Dear Papa had really rather let things run down a bit and the death duties were, of course, absolutely crippling. Once Boys had explained the situation to me I soon realized that the days of having a maid of my own to look after me were dead and gone. Still, we soon found a new job for Miss Marsh and she settled down extraordinarily well selling tickets at the entrance for us. I don't know how she manages so beautifully because, when

I have to do it, I always get terribly muddled with the change. Isn't it funny how ordinary people never seem to have anything less than a pound note in their pockets?' She turned abruptly to her brother. 'Shall I make the cocoa now, Boys, or would you sooner wait a bit?'

'I should make it now, Prissy. I've got a busy afternoon ahead of me – Baker says some of the shells in the grotto are going mouldy – and I'm sure Chief Inspector Dover will want to be getting on, too.'

'Rightie-ho!' Lady Priscilla set off on one of her hand-canters for the kitchen.

Lord Crouch recognized with a sigh that it was now up to him to do the honours. He raised his voice slightly so as to drown the alarming rumbles that had started coming from Dover's stomach. 'Yes, it was indeed a strenuous time but we managed to get things ship-shape in the end. I suppose it was about six months after her return to Beltour that Miss Marsh brought the child, Gary, here. She couldn't continue to live in, of course, but we found her a cottage on the estate. As my sister told you, Miss Marsh said that the child was her sister's illegitimate son but the villagers were soon putting two and two together and performing some simple arithmetical calculations. I'm sorry to say that they came to the conclusion that it was Miss Marsh herself who was Gary's mother and that the boy had been conceived and born during the year that she had been away. Where the real truth lies, I have no idea.'

Dover was rapidly reaching the end of his tether, a feat which didn't take much doing. 'Does it,' he asked, 'make any bloody difference?'

Lord Crouch slowly hunched his shoulders. 'To Gary's murder? Well, I really don't know. All this happened well over twenty years ago and I would have thought that the boy's real parentage had long since ceased to be of much significance. Young Marsh was just an ordinary sort of lad, as far as I am aware. Actually, if you want more information about his recent life, I suggest you have a word with Tiffin.'

Dover was in the middle of an enormous yawn, the compound product of intense boredom and acute under-nourishment, but he interrupted it at the sound of a word which vaguely reminded him of food. 'Tiffin?'

'My butler. The fellow who opened the front door to you.'

'Oh,' said Dover.

'His daughter was engaged to be married to Gary Marsh – though whether that had any bearing on his death either, I'm sure I don't know.'

Three

'Verbal diarrhoea!' snorted Dover viciously. He was so taken with the brilliant originality of the description that he willingly put himself to the trouble of repeating it. 'Bloody verbal diarrhoea!'

MacGregor didn't think this was a very nice way to talk about the sister of a peer but he was reluctant to say so in case he distracted Dover even further from the idea of doing some work by starting an argument. The pair of them had been installed in the Orange Drawing-room, a show apartment which was temporarily closed to the public while the funny smell coming from the fire-place was tracked down and cured. As rooms go, this was lofty, sparsely furnished and as draughty as a football pitch. It also had a very famous painted ceiling with troupes of unclothed ladies and trouserless cherubs which Dover would have instantly condemned as pornographic if he'd been able to see that far.

Showing his usual good taste, MacGregor had settled himself down at a charming little bonheur-du-jour upon which he proceeded to spread out an impressive array of folders and maps. Dover had simply lowered himself into what he judged to be the most comfortable chair in the room. It seemed likely that there would soon be one piece of late eighteenth century Florentine work the less.

MacGregor lovingly opened his first folder. He and Dover were supposed to be planning the details of their forthcoming investigation but privately MacGregor was aiming no higher than ramming enough basic information into his superior's thick skull to stop him making a bigger fool of himself than was necessary.

He cleared his throat. 'Ready, sir?'

'I've been ready for the last bleeding half hour, laddie!' said Dover with his habitual charm of manner.

'Yes, sir. Well, Gary Marsh – the murder victim – was a young man, unmarried, aged twenty-three. He lived here in the village with the maiden aunt who had brought him up since he was a child. He worked as a hotel receptionist in Dunningby, which is a town about twenty miles away. For the past couple of years he's only been at Beltour here for holidays and his off-duty time.'

The Florentine chair creaked violently, indicating that Dover was bestirring himself to ask a question.

MacGregor felt pleased. Such a display of interest was most unusual. 'Sir?'

'What did they give you for lunch at this boozer of yours?'

Oh, well, he should have known better! 'The Bull Reborn, sir? Er,' – MacGregor thought for a moment – 'I had ox-tail soup, steak and kidney pudding, apple pie and fresh cream and some Stilton to finish off with.'

' 'Strewth!' Dover gazed enviously at his sergeant. Some people fell on their feet all right. 'What's the beer like?'

MacGregor was busy running his eye over the reports. 'Oh, not bad, sir. It's quite a decent little pub altogether, really. Now, sir, Gary Marsh was engaged to be married to a local girl called Charmian Tiffin. She's the daughter of....'

'I know all that!' snapped Dover irritably. He remembered the brass-knobbed, broken-springed horror upon which he was expected to rest his weary bones that night. 'Bed all right?'

'I think so, sir.' MacGregor, being young and healthy, didn't pay much attention to these things. Somewhat belatedly he returned the compliment. 'Are you quite comfortable here, sir?'

Dover sank back miserably in his chair. 'Oh, fine,' he said. 'Lap of Luxury.' He hooked another armchair nearer and, with a grunt, hoisted his filthy boots on to its priceless tapestry seat. 'Well, go on!' he rumbled. 'Get on with it! I don't know why you've always got to make such a meal of everything. When was this joker croaked? God rot him!'

'Sunday evening, sir,' said MacGregor, smoothly turning to the right page. 'The local police have been able to fix the time pretty accurately. About half past six.'

'Well, bully for them!' sneered Dover, who knew all about the doctrine of friendly cooperation with provincial police forces and for two pins would have told you where you could stick it. 'I'll lay a pound to a penny they've got it wrong.'

'Oh, I don't think so, sir. Apart from the medical evidence, there's the timetable of Marsh's movements. You see, he was on his way to the railway station to catch the six forty-five back to Dunningby. Now, according to Lord Crouch, he left Beltour House at twenty past six. That would give him about twenty-five minutes, ample time to walk to the. . . .'

'Here, just a minute!' Dover was so excited that he snagged several threads in the tapestry chair seat with the hobnails on his boots. 'Wadderyemean – according to Lord Crouch?'

'Well, sir, it looks very much as though Lord Crouch was the last person to see Gary Marsh alive, apart from the murderer, that is.'

' 'Swelp me!' exclaimed Dover, appalled at the duplicity of mankind. 'There they were, filling me up with all this crap about who What's-his-name's mother really was, but they never so much as mention that His Nibs is suspect number one!'

'Oh, I wouldn't exactly say that, sir!' objected MacGregor quickly. He knew from past experience the danger of letting Dover pick out the murderer before he was even sure of the name of the victim.

'Well, I would! Why hide it, if he's not guilty? I thought there was something shifty about Crouch as soon as I clapped eyes on him. What were him and What's-his-name doing together, anyhow?'

MacGregor would have preferred to deal with things logically and finish detailing the circumstances surrounding the actual murder, but knew the dangers of thwarting the chief inspector. One word out of place and you'd have the old bumbler going to sleep on you. 'I'm not quite sure, sir,' he admitted as he leafed through his reports at top speed. 'Nobody seems to have asked. I gather Lord Crouch tends to get the kid glove treatment in this part of the world.'

Dover sniggered unpleasantly. 'He's in for a nasty shock then, isn't he?' He licked his lips. 'Let's haul him in now and give him a good going-over!'

MacGregor hastened to restrain the savage beast. 'Don't you think it would be a good idea if I finished briefing you first, sir? You'll be in a much better position to put him through it if you have all the facts at your finger-tips.'

Dover's bottom lip protruded sulkily. He was not the man to be bothered about piddling little things like facts but, on the other hand, he didn't care much for indulging in a punch-up on an empty stomach. Typically he extracted a price for his capitulation. 'Got a fag, laddie?' he asked.

MacGregor couldn't help glancing at his watch. At this rate the murderer would be dying of old age before they'd even got around to visiting the scene of the crime. Still – he looked on the bright side – life wasn't entirely without its compensations. 'I'm sorry, sir. We're not allowed to smoke in here.'

Dover's bottom lip jutted out even further. 'Says who?'

'The butler told me, sir. It's something to do with the pictures and the wallpaper. They're afraid of the tobacco smoke damaging them.'

'Stuff that for a tale!' blustered Dover. 'How do you expect me to concentrate without a fag?'

It was an unanswerable question and MacGregor got his cigarette case out. 'I should have thought you'd have been puffing away at one of his lordship's Corona-Coronas, sir!' he joked.

Dover scowled and expelled his first mouthful of smoke straight in his sergeant's face. Manfully MacGregor refrained from ramming the old fool's false teeth straight down his throat and busied himself with finding an ashtray until he'd got his temper back under control.

As far as Dover was concerned, though, honour still wasn't satisfied. He examined with apparent interest the rock crystal bon-bon dish, which was all MacGregor could find, and then deliberately flicked his ash on the carpet. MacGregor gritted his teeth. There is little doubt that if Dover and MacGregor had devoted as much energy and imagination to fighting crime as they did to squabbling with each other, they would both have been considerably more successful in their chosen profession than they were.

MacGregor sat down again and picked up his folder. 'Shall I continue, sir?' he asked icily.

Dover was magnificently indifferent. 'You can stand on your head and wiggle your ears for all I care, laddie.'

'Gary Marsh had been spending the weekend at Beltour, staying as usual with his aunt. A great deal of his time was passed, naturally enough, in his fiancée's company and he'd been to tea at her house on the Sunday afternoon. At about a quarter to six he said goodbye to Miss Tiffin. She knew, it seems, that he was calling on Lord Crouch before catching his train back to Dunningby and she assumed that he would continue from there to the railway station via Bluebell Wood and the Donkey Bridge. It is a recognized short cut, sir.'

Dover sighed and tried to fit himself more comfortably into his protesting chair. Yackety, yackety, yack! All he ever seemed to do, week in and week out, was sit listening to other people flapping their big mouths off. He rested his eyes.

MacGregor ploughed on. It was a lonely furrow. 'The local police – and one is rather inclined to agree with them – think that the murderer knew of Marsh's likely movements and lay in wait for him by the Donkey Bridge. The motive for the crime was not robbery as Marsh's wallet, containing seven pounds, was untouched, and his small suitcase lay unopened in the stream a few feet from the body. Of course, the meeting between Marsh and his assailant could have been purely accidental but the local police doubt it. The short cut is not much frequented, especially when it's getting dark, as it only runs between Beltour House here and the station.'

Dover opened his eyes. 'If there's a railway station that near, why didn't we use it instead of being dumped three miles away?'

'It's only a local line, sir, between Dunningby and Claverhouse. We'd have had to change at Claverhouse and wait nearly two hours for a connection.'

Dover closed his eyes again.

'Well, sir, it would appear that the murderer lay in wait for Gary Marsh at this Donkey Bridge and . . .'

'Hold it!' Every now and again Dover liked to show MacGregor that he was taking an intelligent interest. It helped keep the sergeant on his toes. 'What's to stop the murderer following him from here?'

MacGregor was only too eager to explain. 'Well, partly, sir, because the murder weapon was actually a lump of wood torn off the bridge and partly because of the nature of

Marsh's injuries. You see, the situation is like this, sir: the Donkey Bridge is a rickety little structure crossing a stream in the middle of Bluebell Wood. To get on to the bridge, it seems that you have to negotiate some rather broken, slippery steps. Now, Marsh's body was found in the stream, by the steps on this side of the bridge, and, according to the pathology report, he had been struck down from above. That would imply that the murderer was standing above Marsh, on the bridge presumably, and had attacked him as he was scrambling up these rather awkward steps.'

'Not necessarily,' said Dover.

'Sir?'

'Suppose What's-his-name was a midget and the murderer a great long streak of misery like Lord Crouch? You'd have got the same sort of injuries then, wouldn't you, even if they'd both been standing on the same level?'

'Gary Marsh was six foot one inch tall, sir.'

Once Dover got an idea in his head, it took more than indisputable facts to get it out again. 'So he was bending down tying his bootlaces or something.'

'Well, yes, sir,' admitted MacGregor, hanging on to his reason with both hands, 'I admit that we can't be a hundred per cent sure that the murderer was waiting on the bridge, but it does seem the more likely hypothesis.'

'I'm putting my money on Crouch,' said Dover obstinately. 'He has this meeting with Swamp here, they have a row, he sneaks after him and clobbers him. Plain as the nose on your face! Here, do they still try these bigwigs in the House of Lords?'

MacGregor, unasked, got up and gave Dover another cigarette. He decided to ignore the question about the House of Lords. 'You may be right, sir,' he said, playing it tactfully. 'The trouble is, we are rather working in the dark, aren't we?'

Dover cocked a wary eye. He wasn't usually so alert in the afternoon but the combination of galloping malnutrition and a freezing cold room was playing havoc with his routine.

'I'm sure, sir,' MacGregor went on, trying to introduce the subject as painlessly as possible, 'that we'll have a much clearer idea of what happened when we've seen the actual spot where the murder took place. I was thinking that we might go on out there as soon as we've paid our duty visit to the murder headquarters.'

'Murder headquarters?' Dover was highly indignant. '*This* is the bloody murder headquarters, laddie! Where I am!'

'I meant the one the local police have set up, sir. A temporary centre as near to the scene of the crime as was convenient. They've got everything laid on there, sir – photographs, charts, clerical staff, extra telephones.' MacGregor could see that Dover was not succumbing to the temptations. 'Mr Pinkham, the Chief Constable, promised to meet us there and introduce us to the local chaps.'

'Later,' said Dover. 'Maybe.'

MacGregor smiled a sickly smile. 'Well, actually, sir, he's expecting us in about ten minutes.'

'Hard luck,' said Dover. He settled his head well back and closed his eyes again.

'I really do think, sir, . . .'

'In this weather?' yelped Dover, jerking almost upright in his vexation at the constant badgering. 'It's raining cats and dogs!'

'I've got a car, sir.'

'And me barely out of my sick bed!' remembered Dover, waxing pathetic. 'You want me to catch double pneumonia or something?'

MacGregor would have settled for almost any fatal disease, provided it was sufficiently lingering and painful. 'Perhaps I'd better pop down there by myself, sir, and . . .'

'Your place is with me, laddie! Not that you're any more use than a sick headache but I'm not interviewing Lord Crouch without a reliable witness. If I have to thump him around a bit I want somebody there to swear he attacked me first.'

So much for the sacred obligations of a guest.

MacGregor was spared the embarrassment of wriggling out of this one by a gentle tap on the door. Almost immediately it was opened and Lady Priscilla popped her head round.

'Hello, there!' she hissed. 'How are you getting on?'

Dover responded by promptly turning his face to the wall and it was left to MacGregor to find a suitably evasive, but kindly, answer.

Lady Priscilla needed little encouragement. She advanced a further few inches. 'I've brought you both a nice cup of my herbal tea. It's most refreshing and it helps clear the brain.'

In spite of himself, Dover couldn't resist having a peep. There were three cups on the tray.

'And I wanted to let the chief inspector know about supper,' Lady Priscilla continued, carefully addressing her remarks to MacGregor so as not to disturb the Great Man. 'My brother and I generally have it about seven but, if Mr Dover isn't able to make it by then, it doesn't matter because it's cold. A biscuit, sergeant?'

'Oh, no thank you, Lady Priscilla! I'm afraid I ate far too much at luncheon!' MacGregor, anxious to make a favourable impression, twinkled his eyes roguishly at Lady Priscilla and patted his stomach in a way that wrung Dover's withers.

Lady Priscilla began to pour out her thaumaturgic infusion in a swirl of steam which wouldn't have shamed a Chinese laundry. 'I thought you could take down my statement at the same time,' she said. 'We've got three Darby and Joan coach parties booked for tomorrow and I have to do my stint as a guide. It takes such absolutely ages to get them round, you know. Of course, I don't know anything much about the actual murder but I'm a mine of information about all the circumstances surrounding it – as Chief Inspector Dover will be able to tell you!'

Up to this point Dover had been wavering. After all, nobody likes getting wet and the prospect of tramping round Beltour's draughty acres was not an alluring one. Still, bodily comfort isn't everything. Dover dragged his feet off the chair with the once immaculate tapestry seat and stood up. He jerked his head at MacGregor. 'Come on!'

'Sir?'

Dover looked round for his hat and coat which he had dropped on the floor by the door. 'Mustn't keep the Chief Constable waiting!'

'Oh – no, sir!' MacGregor hastened to pick up Dover's outer garments though normally he was careful to avoid touching them with his bare hands. He threw an apologetic smile at Lady Priscilla. 'I'm afraid we shall have to postpone our interview until later.'

Dover let MacGregor stuff him into his overcoat. 'Tell her I shan't be in for supper!' he instructed in a raucous stage whisper.

'Sir?'

'Tell her I shan't be in to supper, you moron!' repeated Dover hoarsely as he grabbed his bowler hat. 'I'm eating with you tonight. Tell her we've got to go to a bloody conference or something!'

Four

'That broken-down rabbit-hutch?'

In spite of the fact that he was drenched to the skin, Mr Pinkham could feel his face burning. To hear the luxury, jumbo-sized caravan, which had been specially hired at great expense for the occasion, sneeringly disparaged as a rabbit-hutch was really more than flesh and blood should be expected to endure.

Dover, still ensconced in the back seat of the car which had been placed at his disposal, elaborated gleefully on his original observation. 'Or a chicken-coop! Yes, that's it – a chicken-coop that some stupid idiot's dumped down in the middle of a bloody bog!' He glared pointedly at the Chief Constable who was standing with MacGregor by the car door. They had both been standing there for some time as they tried to entice Dover into getting out and braving the elements.

Had Mr Pinkham been in a more amiable frame of mind, even he would have been forced to admit that the prospect before them was not an inviting one. In the middle distance lay Bluebell Wood, its woebegone, dripping trees hiding the fatal Donkey Bridge and the stream it spanned from view. Between the wood and the narrow private road on which Dover's car stood was a spacious, grassy meadow and it was in the middle of this meadow that the Chief Constable had established his temporary murder headquarters. He had been guided, perhaps, more by romanticism than by an appreciation of what was practicable. The meadow was a picturesque spot, much favoured by visitors to Beltour for alfresco meals and carefree frolics. The picnickers, however, only flocked to deposit their litter about the sward on fine, warm days in the height of summer. On wet, cold days in the depths of winter nobody but a dedicated masochist who got his kicks out of wet feet would have dreamed of venturing there.

'I've got a spare pair of gum boots for you,' said the Chief Constable.

Dover curled his lip eloquently and pulled his overcoat collar up round his ears.

The caravan stood in the middle of the meadow with the rain beating a relentless devil's tattoo on the plywood roof. A large number of thick cables, already sinking deep in the mire, snaked away to the edge of the meadow where they disappeared into the undergrowth. Human interest was provided by a couple of uniformed constables who were sheltering as best they could under the canopy of some bare trees and squelching miserably from one muddy boot to the other. Even further off, under another clump of trees, a handful of very lowly representatives of the mass media were sullenly cursing their luck and passing a hip flask round. They knew that, miracles and extensive bribery apart and notwithstanding Lord Crouch's hopes, nobody was going to print or screen anything more about the Beltour murder mystery. It had had all the marks of a dead duck, newswise, from the very beginning and it was only the unexpected arrival of Scotland Yard that had revived this last flicker of interest.

Members of the general public, supposedly so avid for

ghoulish sensations, were noteworthy only by their total absence but on the horizon some spectators were approaching. Beltour was famous (in certain admittedly restricted circles) for its herd of the rare Grevy's zebra and a scattering of these animals now came slowly over the hill. Known to local wits as the Beltour United, they were doubtless recalling happier and sunnier days when potato crisps and iced lollies were to be scrounged for the asking.

'That might make a good picture,' one of the TV reporters observed to his cameraman. He tried it out. 'A weirdly exotic note is struck . . .'

'Oh, balls!' said the cameraman and sneezed for the tenth time without benefit of handkerchief. 'Jesus, do you think the fuzz are going to stand out there all effing day?'

No, they weren't. Dover had finally succumbed to the blandishments and, under the solemn promise of a scalding hot cup of tea with fruit cake, was graciously allowing MacGregor to put the gum boots on for him. Another few minutes and Dover was actually embarking on the hundred yard walk to the caravan with his two companions supporting him on either side. The TV cameraman withdrew back to the trunk of his tree and lowered his camera. 'If I shot that,' he remarked righteously, 'the confidence of the British People in the police forces of this country would be permanently undermined.'

A nearby sound engineer agreed. 'Always provided that they didn't mistake that old pig-in-the-middle for a cow elephant on her way to the labour ward,' he said and chucked an empty cigarette packet at the leading zebra which was coming far too close. The zebra ate the cigarette packet and stood hopefully waiting for more.

Back on the front where it was all happening, things had ground to a halt once more while Dover examined the little flight of wooden steps up which he and his seventeen and a quarter stone were supposed to mount.

'I'll go first, shall I?' asked Mr Pinkham, anxious to ensure that everybody inside the caravan was looking suitably happy and busy.

'If I come a cropper,' Dover warned MacGregor in a low, intense growl, 'I'll break every bone in your miserable body!'

MacGregor decided to take the risk and, by exerting himself above and beyond the call of duty, eventually managed to propel his chief inspector up the steps and get him poised in the open doorway. Dover was granted just enough time to appreciate the tableau vivant which had been so carefully laid on for him. Two young detective constables, heads together, were frowning in impressive concentration at the sheet of blank paper spread out over their football pools. A uniformed sergeant stood poised by a filing cabinet, into whose half-opened drawer he had just dropped his wad of chewing gum. Over in the far corner a rosy-cheeked police cadet thrashed away at a typewriter and wasted a perfectly good report form by pounding 'a quick brown fox' all over it. Strategically placed in the foreground was a policewoman, the prettiest in the force. She flashed a dazzling smile at Dover, threw her chest out and raised her teapot on high.

For a moment everybody stood and gawped at each other. Then the telephone began ringing and the Chief Constable who had been expecting it (and had personally arranged it) leapt forward eagerly to snatch up the receiver.

And that did it.

The caravan had never been designed to have the best part of half a ton of humanity milling around inside it and its somewhat flimsy foundations had already been seriously undermined by forty-eight hours of continual rain. Mr Pinkham's enthusiastic plunge from one end of the caravan to the other proved to be the final straw which tipped the scales. There was a sudden lurch and, amidst some surprisingly hysterical screaming and shouting, everything and everybody began sliding down the slippery slope which fell away from north to south. There was much democratic mingling of tumbling bodies, much flailing of arms and legs, a great deal of cracking of heads. Desks, filing cabinets, trestle tables and typewriters crashed down into the pit. The large pot of freshly made tea, plus a trayful of cups and saucers went inexorably after them.

But what of our hero's fate? Not actually being inside the caravan when it tipped, Dover was only thrown off balance and merely descended the little flight of wooden steps somewhat more speedily and awkwardly than he had gone up them. Compared to the others, he came off very well. The meadow was a quagmire with the consistency of a rather milky rice pudding and Dover landed in it with a squelch. He was a little shocked and a little winded but, otherwise, quite unharmed. After a moment's pause his indignant howls joined and overwhelmed the cries coming from inside the collapsed caravan.

MacGregor had simply stepped back on to the grass when he felt the caravan begin to go. Faced now with what might turn out to be quite a nasty accident, he swung into action right away and rushed to Dover's prostrate form.

Away under the sheltering trees, the callous delight of the gentlemen from TV and the press was only slightly marred by them having the herd of zebras scampering away in panic through their midst. A young cub reporter from the local newspaper started forward eagerly, his notebook at the ready. The television cameraman hauled him back.

'Save your energy, son,' he advised.

'But it's the story of the year! That's the Chief Constable himself in there, never mind the top brass from Scotland Yard. Come on, Jacko,' – he appealed to his pimply photographer – 'we'll make the front page of the nationals with this!'

The TV cameraman maintained his hold. 'You try splashing that, son, and your life won't be worth living. They'll lean on you so hard it'll make a pile driver look like a bloody feather duster.'

'But ...'

'Cool it, kid! The fuzz never did have much of a sense of humour.'

By now the police were starting to extricate themselves from the wreckage and there was much examining of bruises and licking of wounds. Nobody had been hurt but everybody, especially the senior ranks, felt that they had been made to look ridiculous. The Chief Constable in particular was not quite speechless with fury. He'd got the best part of the contents of the milk jug over his best tunic and his silver braided peak cap was a complete write-off. He rounded on the uniformed sergeant who was mopping at a bleeding nose and feeling sorry for himself. 'I'll have somebody's head for this!' he promised savagely and splashed off across the grass to see what had happened to Dover.

MacGregor had managed to turn the body over and Dover was reclining on his back. His eyes were closed but, with the rain lashing down on his face, it was obvious he was about to stage a swift recovery.

He stuck to the well-worn script. 'Where am I?' he groaned.

Mr Pinkham gazed down at him. 'Well, at least he's not dead.'

'No,' said MacGregor, who'd had his moment of hope.

'Do you think it would be safe to try and move him?'

Provided the crane could take the weight, thought MacGregor unkindly. 'Oh, I should think so, sir,' he said aloud. 'Perhaps some of your chaps could help cart him over to the car?'

Dover waited until as many hands as could be mustered had raised him up before fluttering his eyelids. With a pathetic gesture he clutched at MacGregor's sleeve. 'Don't take me back to Beltour!' he begged, and the bowler hat some idiot had placed on his chest like an inverted chamber pot heaved with emotion. 'Take me to the village pub! I'll rest easier there.' His eyelids slowly dropped again.

'Funny thing to say,' grunted the Chief Constable as the

cortège staggered off across the grass. 'I suppose he doesn't want to put Lord Crouch and Lady Priscilla to any trouble. Very considerate!'

MacGregor, po-faced, agreed that it was.

The Bull Reborn was, as MacGregor had indicated, quite a nice little pub, but 'little' was the operative word. It only boasted three bedrooms and had been turning business away ever since those two village kids had discovered Gary Marsh's body lying face down in the stream.

'He'll have to double up with you,' the landlord told MacGregor as he served Dover with a hot toddy. 'These reporter fellows don't seem to know when they'll be going and they're already sleeping three to a bed. I couldn't squeeze so much as a church mouse in till they've gone.'

MacGregor swallowed hard. 'Couldn't you possibly ...'

The landlord shook his head. 'I've told you, sergeant. Sorry. Besides, you'll be all right! That old couch in your room is a sight more comfortable than it looks.'

Dover passed his empty glass back. 'I may need a bit of nursing during the night,' he pointed out weakly. 'Just for the first few days.' He looked round the bar parlour with considerable satisfaction. A log fire crackling in the hearth, cosy chairs, a congenial atmosphere and ample supplies of booze just across the old oak counter. Who said everything didn't turn out for the best?

He felt in such a good mood that he was even willing to let MacGregor go off and do a bit of detecting on his own. Owing to the difficulty of negotiating the stairs, Dover himself had decided to remain on the ground floor until he'd had his dinner – a treat to which he was looking forward with dribbling anticipation.

When MacGregor had taken his leave, the landlord – a man with a heart of pure gold and his own reasons for sucking up to the cops – brought Dover another steaming glass of the stuff that not only cheers but inebriates as well and settled himself down on the other side of the fireplace.

'You'll have found 'em a queer lot, I'll be bound,' he said as a large ginger cat glided silently up onto his knees. 'Up at Beltour. Lord Crouch and his sister.'

Dover cautiously agreed that queer was probably as good a description as any.

' 'Course, we're used to 'em,' said the landlord. 'Nothing they do would ever surprise me, specially since they opened the place to the public. Gone mad, I reckon. Bloody zebras in the park – well, I ask you! I did hear as how they was thinking of getting a couple of camels and a baby elephant for rides in the rose garden. They must be making a mint of money, what with one thing and another. Do you know how many set teas they sold last year? Thirty-six thousand! Just you think of the profit on that! And now they've had this blooming murder. That'll put their takings up. There's not many stately homes with their own murder, is there? There was a chap in the bar last night as reckoned old Crouch was going to set up a sort of Madame Tussauds thing down by the Donkey Bridge. You know – wax models. Gary Marsh being struck down by his murderer. 'Course, they'll have to wait until your lot find out who did it, won't they?'

'Got any ideas?' asked Dover, who didn't mind picking somebody else's brains just to be sociable.

The landlord shook his head. 'No, it's a right mystery, believe me! I mean, young Marsh was such an ordinary sort of chap. Harmless enough, I should have thought. I can't think what anybody'd get out of killing him.'

'What's the connection between him and Lord Crouch?'

The landlord shot Dover a sly glance. He'd need to watch his step with this one. Fat, thick looking lump the fellow might be, but there were no flies on him. 'Well, now, that's a bit of a mystery, too. Not that there hasn't been a fair bit of speculation about it over the years.' He chuckled. 'That old bar there could tell a few tales out of school, believe me it could!'

Dover settled back in his chair.

The landlord tossed another log on the fire. 'What you've got to realize, Mr Dover, is that Beltour is a pretty compact little community. Oh, it's beginning to break up now, I grant you, but we still all live very much in the shadow of the Big House. Why, I guarantee there's not a single family in this village that doesn't depend one way or the other on Lord Crouch for its living. I do myself! My bread and butter trade comes from the chaps that work for the estate and my jam comes from the visitors. And what are the visitors visiting? Beltour House, that's what. They wouldn't come within a hundred miles, otherwise. So, you see, we've got ties here and it's not easy for people from outside to get themselves integrated, as you might say. Not that there haven't always been plenty of strangers knocking around. French chefs and ladies-maids, Irish grooms, footmen with black faces and posh butlers from London. In the old days I reckon all the upper servants were foreigners of one sort or another. Now, Milly Marsh – that's young Gary's auntie – she came in that category. Personal maid to Lady Priscilla, she was, and a right pretty girl in those days. Milly Marsh, that is. Lady Priscilla's never been much of a sight for sore eyes. Well, there was quite a few of the local lads as had their eye on Milly Marsh but, somehow, she just wasn't interested. Stand-offish, they called her.

'By gosh,' – the landlord broke off and smacked his lips – 'but talking's thirsty work, isn't it?' He gently eased the ginger cat off his knees and got up. 'I'll not be a minute!'

He went behind the bar and the ginger cat attempted to climb into Dover's lap. It got a smart punch in the whiskers for its presumption.

A moment or two later and the landlord was back again, two foaming tankards of beer in his hands. 'There you are, sir! I trust you'll find it to your taste. Good health!'

Dover raised his tankard in comradely salute. He was

really beginning to take quite a fancy to the hospitable licensee of The Bull Reborn. The landlord didn't think things were going too badly, either. Only the ginger cat, sulking on the hearth rug, was less than satisfied with his lot.

Five

'Aye, Milly Marsh,' said the landlord, coming up for air with a burp Dover wouldn't have been ashamed of. 'Well, like I was saying, the general opinion round here was that she gave herself airs. Snooty, you know. Anyways, our home-grown Romeos soon remembered that there were more fish in the sea and gradually lost interest. Then, when old Lord Crouch kicked the bucket – drank like a fish, he did, without a word of a lie – and they shut Beltour up for a year, we all thought we'd seen the last of her. But, no – back she comes when they took up residence again and gets a nice bit of promotion into the bargain because that's when they went public, you know, and young Milly stops being a servant and becomes a cashier, no less.

'Well, life settled down again, though it took us a while to get used to the present Lord Crouch and all the cars and motor coaches that started streaming through the village. Milly Marsh hadn't changed, though. She still kept all us muck-spreading yokels at arm's length. Specially the men – and she wasn't over-friendly with the women, either. Then this blooming baby arrives out of the blue. "My sister's child," says Milly Marsh. "Ho ho!" says us. "Now pull the other one!" '

Dover had finished his beer. He put his tankard down with a loud bang. 'Oh, yes,' he said, always prepared to pinch somebody else's punch line, 'I'd heard a lot of people thought Miss Marsh was the kid's mother.'

The landlord, who enjoyed quite a reputation as a raconteur, was justifiably annoyed and made a mental note to put both the toddy and the two beers down on this paunchy old bluebottle's bill. 'Well, yes,' he admitted, 'that's what everybody reckoned at first. We all thought she'd pushed off up north or wherever it was, had a tumble in the hay and been left holding the baby. Of course, it'd have looked a sight too obvious if she'd brought the kid with her when she came back, so she waits a few months and then tries to palm it off on a sister nobody's ever heard of. Well, nobody round here was going to have the wool pulled over their eyes like that and there was a fair amount of sniggering over how Miss High and Mighty had finally come a proper cropper. Then, as time went by, people found other things to gossip about and young Gary grew up like just any other kid, no better and no worse, if you ask me.' The landlord took a long swig at his beer. 'Mind you, all this happened a long time ago but I reckon it must have been round about the time Gary started going to school that the second batch of rumours started.'

'Oh, yes?' Dover was feeling decidedly sleepy but he didn't want to drop off in case another pint of best bitter should be forthcoming. 'You got any cigarettes behind that bar of yours?'

'Of course. What sort do you want?'

'Oh, something king-size,' said Dover expansively. 'Give us fifty of the best you've got, and a couple of boxes of matches.'

'Do you want to pay cash or shall I book 'em for you?'

'Stick 'em on my sergeant's bill,' said Dover. 'In fact,

anything I have you can stick on his bill.'

The landlord registered mild surprise.

'It makes it easier when we're claiming our expenses,' explained Dover with a grin that would have made the most gullible of mugs uneasy. 'Now, you were saying?'

'Eh? Oh, about the new set of rumours?' The landlord's eyes sparkled as he handed the cigarettes over and sat down again. 'Well, they were pretty juicy, I can tell you. The word went round like wildfire that young Gary was actually Lady Priscilla's little bastard!'

'Go on!' chuckled Dover, dropping his extinguished, though still hot, match on the ginger cat in his delight.

'I thought that'd make you open your eyes! Yes, well, you see – Lady Priscilla had always taken quite a lot of interest in the kid, though it's obvious she's not much of a one for children. She puts a good face on it at speech days and sports days and such like but a blind man could see she's not the maternal type. But, where Gary Marsh was concerned, things were different. For instance, she found Milly Marsh that cottage on the estate, got her a better job, kept giving her bits of things for the baby. I did hear as how she'd offered to send Gary away to a posh school but Milly Marsh didn't want to part with him. Well, you can't be surprised if the tongues started wagging, can you? And, you see, the timing fitted Lady Priscilla just as snugly as it did Milly Marsh. Lady Priscilla had spent a whole year away from Beltour, hadn't she? Sailing round the world or some such rubbish. Well, it wouldn't be the first time that some well-born young lady's been shipped off on an extended holiday to get over a temporary embarrassment, would it? Why, there's even some who reckoned it all happened here at Beltour and that was really why they closed the house in the first place. You could take your choice as to who the father was, but most people put their money on an under-gardener they had working there about that time. Good looking young spark, he was, and left a few aching hearts here in the village when he was sacked with a month's wages in lieu of notice. So, you see, everything fitted together, neat as a jig-saw puzzle. And Milly Marsh could be trusted to keep a secret, specially if she was being well paid for it. Of course, nowadays, girls'd just brazen it out if they wanted to keep the kid with 'em, but they didn't twenty odd years ago. Twenty years ago people still had a sense of what was decent. Mind you,' – the landlord glanced up at the clock and got reluctantly to his feet – 'I'm just telling you what the local gossip is. And now, if you'll excuse me, I've got some work to do. Opening time doesn't wait for anyone. Do you fancy a refill before I go?'

Dover remained by the fire until dinner time, dozing in the snug warmth, drinking and dribbling over the menu. By the time the enormous, stomach distending meal he had ordered for himself was ready, there was still no sign of MacGregor. Dover didn't bother waiting for him but took himself off to the little dining room and was soon stuffing himself with as much satisfying stodge as he could get his teeth round. That nasty, rabbit-food luncheon at Beltour House was soon no more than a faint, nauseating memory.

All around Dover in the dining room the reporters covering the murder were cheerfully and noisily scoffing down everything that was put in front of them. They had been just as cheerful and noisy in the bar earlier and although one or two speculative glances had been cast at Dover, deep and somnolent in his chair by the fire, nobody had actually approached him. This was not from fear or any sense of diffidence but simply because Dover's reputation had preceded him.

'There's no point in asking *him* for any information,' the cynical TV cameraman had proclaimed as he reached for his fourth double gin. 'He knows about as much of what's going on as that bloody ginger tom-cat does. Probably less.'

The cub reporter from the local rag wasn't so sure. He sipped his medium sweet cider with the air of a man of the world. 'Maybe he's a thinker,' he said. 'Maybe he just sits there like a spider in the middle of its web, gathering all the strands of information together and weaving them into . . .'

The cameraman let out a scornful bark of a laugh. 'If you believe that, you'll believe anything! Take it from me, son, all that old boozer uses his head for is somewhere to stick his hat. And the next time you find yourself in a public library, get yourself a book on arachnology!'

'Eh?'

The cameraman turned away to find a more congenial companion. 'Because you know even less about bloody spiders than you do about old Dover there!'

MacGregor came panting into the dining room just as Dover was shovelling most of the contents of the cheese board on to his plate. 'Ah, there you are, sir! Er – are you feeling better?'

Dover raised a face flushed with over-indulgence. 'Not so's you'd notice,' he rumbled. 'I'm going straight to bed as soon as I've finished my supper. You can give us a hand upstairs.'

'Of course, sir!' MacGregor turned with thankfulness away from the guzzling on the other side of the table to exercise his charm on the waitress who had arrived to take his order. 'I'll have . . .'

'We've kept your dinner warm for you,' interrupted the totally unimpressed young lady. 'You don't mind if I bring it in all at once, do you? Only I'm due off in five minutes.'

Congealed sheep's brains is not to every man's taste and was so little so on this occasion that, for once in his life, even Dover balked at gobbling up his sergeant's leftovers.

It was only later when he was tucked up in MacGregor's bed and sipping a double nightcap that Dover bethought himself to ask what his underling had been up to.

'Oh, nothing very much,' said MacGregor as he cleared the chinaware away from the old-fashioned wash-stand which he was hoping to use as a desk. 'The light won't worry you, will it, sir?'

'Yes, it will!' said Dover who didn't see any point in beating about the bush where his personal comfort was concerned. 'What have you been doing?'

'Well, I went back to the temporary murder headquarters, sir, and gave them a hand with the clearing up there. There wasn't much real damage actually and, once we'd got the caravan back on an even keel, everything could have carried on as before. But the Chief Constable wasn't too keen. He decided that he could run things just as well from Claverhouse, especially since you and I were on hand down here.'

Dover showed his unerring sense for the unimportant once again. 'Where's Claverhouse?' he demanded.

'It's the town we arrived at, sir. The one with the railway station. It's got a biggish police station as well and, from now on, the local police will be working from there.'

'Good,' grunted Dover. 'It'll keep 'em out of my hair. Well?'

'Sir?'

'You were on the loose for the best part of four hours, laddie and I'm still waiting to hear what you were doing. You're being bloody cagey about it. What are you hiding?'

'Nothing, sir. I gave them a hand with the caravan and then I had to go over to Beltour House and collect your things and explain about the accident and everything.'

'That'd have taken me four minutes!' sneered Dover.

'Well, after that, sir, I helped them pack up all the stuff that had been in the caravan and take it back to Claverhouse.' MacGregor saw the look on Dover's face and was stung to defend himself. 'Well, we do have to work with them don't we sir? I thought if I gave them a bit of a helping hand, now, it might pay dividends later.'

'Crawler!' said Dover. 'You're a right mug, you are! God help us the day we need anything from that bunch of country bumpkins! As a matter of fact, I'm already well on the way to solving this case by my own *unaided* efforts.' He glanced at MacGregor to see if this subtle shaft had gone home. 'Well, go on! What else?'

'That really took up most of the time, sir. Oh, well, when we'd finished, Inspector Dawkins did stand me a couple of jars.'

'Ah,' said Dover, nodding his head sagely and addressing the ceiling, 'now we're getting down to it! And who's Inspector Dawkins when he's at home?'

MacGregor began unloading the contents of his briefcase onto the cleared surface of the wash-stand. 'He's the local CID inspector who was in charge of the investigation before we arrived, sir. I found his comments on the case very useful. You see, he is quite convinced that the killer is a local man.'

'So am I!' snapped Dover.

MacGregor could see that Lord Crouch was about to raise his ugly head again and resolutely went on talking. 'The point is, sir, that Inspector Dawkins thinks that only a local man would have known about that path to the railway station through Bluebell Wood. He also believes that the crime was probably premeditated because nobody, coming *away* from the railway station, could have had any reason to be on the path at that time. And, if it was premeditated, that points even more to a local man because only a local man would have known that he could tear a lump of wood off the bridge to use as a weapon. It looks to me like a reasonable working hypothesis.'

'Could still have been a homicidal tramp,' grumbled Dover, sticking a spoke in for the sheer hell of it.

'It could, sir.' Since MacGregor was having to share a bedroom with Dover he was more inclined than usual to humour the old fool. 'On the other hand, there aren't really all that number of homicidal tramps knocking around these days, are there? Certainly there's been nobody of anything approaching that description seen anywhere in the neighbourhood of Beltour.'

Dover's mind had already flitted off to a happier topic and he rattled his brandy glass against the bedhead. MacGregor obediently came over to relieve his master of the burden.

'Are you going to lie down now, sir?'

'Not that I'll be able to sleep,' came the surly response as Dover sank down under the bedclothes with all the grace of a torpedoed ironclad. 'I've had a busy evening, too, you know!' he remembered, poking his head up out of the blankets. 'I haven't been sitting around on my backside, twiddling my thumbs, like some I could name.'

'No, sir.'

'Fr'instance,' Dover went on, 'did you know it's quite on the cards that Lady Priscilla is Gary Marsh's mother?'

'No, sir, I didn't. But I'm not really surprised.'

'Oh?'

'Well, sir, I have suspected all along that Lord Crouch and his sister probably had some ulterior motive for inviting you to stay at Beltour. Obviously they knew all about the mystery surrounding Marsh's birth and they wanted to get their version in first. Not that I think Gary Marsh's parentage is of any importance to our enquiries.'

'You don't?'

'Good heavens, no, sir! Why on earth should it have?'

Dover didn't know so he changed the subject. 'Are you going to keep that light on all blooming night?'

'I'll shade it, sir.'

Dover sniffed loudly and then thought of something else. 'I want a glass of water!' he whined.

'Of course, sir!' MacGregor poured out a glass from the carafe which he had tidied away on to the floor. 'Here you are!'

He closed his eyes as Dover solemnly dropped both sets of his false teeth into the proffered tumbler.

'And don't droth 'em!' came the lisped instruction.

MacGregor got a grip on himself. 'I'll put them here on your bedside table, sir.'

'Yeth, you do thath.'

MacGregor then returned to his wash-stand and, sitting down, picked up a sheet of paper and began to read it.

Dover moved around restlessly as his digestive juices fought it out with the gargantuan meal which had just been wolfed down so mercilessly. 'Whath'th that?' he demanded fretfully over the gurglings of his guts.

'Just the log the local police kept, sir,' said MacGregor, praying that Dover wasn't going to go on nattering all night. It was getting late and MacGregor was counting on snatching a few hours of sleep himself before facing the rigours of yet another day with Scotland Yard's most unwanted man. It was then that pure inspiration struck. If there was one thing guaranteed to send Dover speeding off to the Land of Nod ... 'I'll give you the gist of it, shall I, sir?'

There was an unintelligible grunt and some twanging of springs from the bed.

MacGregor smiled grimly to himself and settled back in his chair. 'Gary Marsh's body,' he began in a dull, monotonous voice, 'was initially discovered in the stream by the Donkey Bridge by two small boys, namely Angus Gideon Kemble and George Tupper – both aged ten. On Monday morning – that is, the day after the murder – they were, I regret to say, playing truant from school and had gone to Bluebell Wood to fish for sticklebacks and frog spawn. They came across the body at about ten o'clock and were luckily far too scared to go near it or touch anything. Unluckily, they were also frightened of contacting anybody about it in case they got into trouble for playing truant. They ran off and then hung around in another part of the park, arguing about what, if anything, they should do. In the end their public spirit prevailed. They sneaked into the village and tried to make an anonymous 999 call from the public phone box. The operator at the other end was naturally extremely suspicious, especially as the kids refused to give their names and addresses, so he kept them talking and alerted a patrol car which happened to be in the area. The boys made their emergency call at 10.47 and were apprehended running away from the telephone kiosk by the occupants of the patrol car at 10.52.

'At 11.00 hours precisely, finally convinced by the boys that this was not a leg-pull, Constable Muldoon set off for the Donkey Bridge, arriving there at 11.17. Once there he ascertained that there was, indeed, a body and that, to the best of his knowledge, it was dead. At 11.29 he radioed back to his headquarters ...'

MacGregor let his voice trail softly away and listened for a few seconds to the steady snores coming from the bed. It had worked! He put the log sheet to one side and, not without a deep sigh of self pity, unscrewed his pen and got down to the tricky business of writing a report which, without actually lying, implied that considerably more progress had been made than was, in fact, the case.

Six

On the following morning Dover woke up in what was for
him a spanking good humour. A square meal and a sound
sleep (broken only by the odd nocturnal trip to the bathroom) had done wonders for his morale and now he'd got
breakfast to look forward to. MacGregor, on the other hand,
was in very poor shape. He had not anticipated that sharing
a bedroom with Dover was going to be any picnic but the
reality had proved even more gruesome than his worst fears.
He had worked away conscientiously at his wash-stand
until two o'clock and then climbed wearily into his makeshift
bed on the sofa. Three hours later he was still trying to get
to sleep. The broken springs, the mysterious lump in the
small of his back – these he could have coped with. Even
Dover's lusty and unremitting snores might have been
sublimated by the exercise of will power. What MacGregor
couldn't ignore were the frantic sallies down the corridor to
the loo. When Dover felt uncomfortable he liked everyone
around him to suffer, too. No sooner, it seemed, had
MacGregor sunk into a shallow doze than a hellish cacophony
of grunts and curses broke out. The light was switched on
and the groans and oaths increased as Dover struggled into

his overcoat and went crashing out of the door. The walls of The Bull Reborn were thin and MacGregor was spared nothing as he lay waiting for the flushing of the cistern which heralded Dover's equally blasphemous and noisy return. Sometimes there were variations on the basic disturbance as when other roused sleepers bawled obscene suggestions from their beds or as when Dover paused to poke MacGregor into complete wakefulness in order to advise him to give thanks for a healthy bladder.

MacGregor, then, faced the new day with a furred tongue and a splitting headache. At breakfast he toyed half-heartedly with a piece of dry toast while Dover joyously shovelled down everything in sight.

When the only food left unconsumed was the lump of marmalade oozing gently down Dover's waistcoat, the chief inspector lit up one of MacGregor's cigarettes and undid the top button of his trousers with a smile of perfect bliss. 'Well, now,' he boomed, 'this won't buy the baby a new frock!'

MacGregor tried unsuccessfully to focus his aching eyes. 'I beg your pardon, sir?'

'Out and about, laddie! That's where we ought to be – out and about!'

MacGregor repressed a shudder. 'I thought you'd prefer to take things easy today, sir. After your accident ...'

'Nonsense! A breath of fresh air'll do me the world of good.'

Dover's unwonted heartiness was making MacGregor feel quite ill. 'If you say so, sir.'

Dover was about to make some invidious comparison between himself and the effete examples of modern youth with whom he was lumbered when he caught sight of the ginger cat staring balefully at him round the dining room door. Well, Dover didn't take looks like that from anybody, never mind some moth-eaten old moggie that should have gone into the canal with a brick round its neck years ago. He picked up the empty toast rack and took careful aim. The ginger cat didn't wait to see if Dover could throw straight but took to its heels with a long drawn out miaow of terror.

'Coward!' jeered Dover.

MacGregor watched this performance with apathetic resignation. He'd seen Dover making a public spectacle of himself too often to get all hot and bothered about a minor incident like this. He pushed his teacup away. 'What were you intending to do exactly, sir?'

'Go and ask a few questions, of course! What else, moron?'

MacGregor rested his head on his hands and thought about death. 'Who were you thinking of tackling first, sir?'

'Good God!' roared Dover. 'Do I have to make all the bloody decisions round here?'

MacGregor flinched at the noise but he pulled himself together. 'I think that perhaps the Tiffins are the ones we should interview first, sir. With Miss Tiffin being engaged to . . .'

A sensible suggestion was all Dover had been waiting for. 'We'll go and see that spinster aunt!' he announced. 'Fetch the car round to the front while I nip into the gents!'

Miss Milly Marsh's cottage was only a few minutes drive away so Dover consented to sit in front next to MacGregor. He was in a very sociable mood that morning. 'Do they still hang lords with a silken rope?' he asked chattily as MacGregor slipped the car into gear.

MacGregor stifled a groan. Of all the damn-fool things to say! 'No, sir. And, frankly, I doubt if they ever did. I think it's just one of these myths, you know.'

Dover scowled. Toffee-nosed young pup!

'In any case, sir,' – MacGregor turned the car at the top of the village street – 'nobody gets hanged with any kind of rope these days.'

'More's the pity!' grunted Dover. 'The country's gone to the dogs since those gibbering idiots abolished capital punishment. Every spotty-faced yobbo that goes robbing telephone boxes carries a gun. Why shouldn't they? Ten measly years in the nick doesn't worry anybody. No, the only language those murdering bastards understand is the good old eight o'clock walk and the knot tucked behind their left ear. Not a deterrent? You should have seen their faces in the old days when the judge put the black cap on! That'd have shown you whether hanging put the wind up 'em or not! And then there's the cat!' Dover's eyes misted over nostalgically as he thought about the cat. 'That's something else that wants bringing back. A dozen or so lashes with a cat-o'-nine-tails and some of these young thugs we have to deal with would soon . . . *What the hell*!' The brim of Dover's bowler fetched up with a sharp smack against the windscreen.

Totally unrepentant, MacGregor dragged on the hand brake and switched off the ignition. 'We're there, sir,' he said.

Miss Marsh was a short, heavily built woman with a discontented face. Twenty years ago she might have been pretty but it was hard now to see in her the girl the landlord remembered. She was dressed in black and received the visit of the police with the same tight-lipped stoicism with which she met all the other misfortunes that life inflicted upon her.

Dover and MacGregor were conducted into the front parlour. It was a cold, musty room. The curtains were drawn too but Miss Marsh made no move to open them. Evidently she considered that the eerie gloaming was more than good enough for her callers and, in any case, there was plenty of light for them to make out their surroundings. The furnishings of the room struck a suitably lugubrious note. A large, highly polished table had been dragged into the middle of the room and its top cleared of all encumbrances. It stood there, empty and all too obviously waiting. Two somewhat premature wreaths were propped one on either side of the fireplace while, on the mantelpiece, the framed photograph of a callow-looking youth was already draped with crepe.

Miss Marsh surveyed the scene with bleak satisfaction. 'He'd sooner go from here,' she announced.

'Er – quite,' agreed MacGregor, looking almost as awkward as he felt.

'I shall give him a good funeral. I didn't skimp him in life and I shan't skimp him in death. And folks needn't think it's coming out of his insurance money, either. That's all going towards his headstone. I'm not going to have them saying round here that I didn't do right by him, even though he did bring shame on my name both coming into this world and going out of it.'

MacGregor didn't fail to notice that Dover seemed to have suddenly lost his tongue. The chief inspector was just standing there, gazing longingly at a couple of stiff-backed chairs pushed up against the wall but, for once in his life, not daring to go and sit down on one of them uninvited.

MacGregor drew what little pleasure he could out of that situation and turned back to Miss Marsh, feeling that her rather enigmatic remarks could not be allowed to go unchallenged. 'How do you mean,' he asked hesitantly, 'brought shame on your name?'

Miss Marsh peered sourly at him in the twilight. 'Don't tell me you didn't know Gary was illegitimate,' she said. 'I'll bet they couldn't wait to let you know all about that down in the village. Not that I ever made any secret about it. It was something Gary had to learn to live with and the sooner he started the better. I don't hold with sweeping things under the carpet. Gary used to come home from school sometimes, crying because the other kids had been calling him names. I always told him how lucky he was. He'd got the chance to find out right at the beginning of his life what suffering shameless immorality brings in its wake. "You're learning your lesson early," I used to tell him. "Just see that you profit by it and I shall be more than satisfied." '

'But, what was shameful about his death?' asked MacGregor, more than a little put out of his stride by Miss Marsh's grim philosophy.

Miss Marsh bristled with astonishment. 'You don't call being murdered a shameful way to go? Well, young man, I certainly do! All the gossip, things in the newspapers and on the television, policemen tramping in and out and poking their noses into everything! It's an ordeal I wouldn't wish on my worst enemy. I can tell you, since this business happened I've prayed every night for a decent and respectable death when my time comes.'

MacGregor took a deep breath. 'I see,' he said. 'Well, Miss Marsh, I wonder if you could tell us something about your – er – nephew. What sort of a person was he?'

'A miserable sinner,' said Miss Marsh mechanically, 'like the rest of us.'

Whatever control MacGregor had ever had on the situation was beginning to slip. 'You mean he'd been in trouble with the police?' he asked stupidly.

'I certainly do not! He'd have found no shelter under my roof if there'd been any goings on of that kind!'

MacGregor managed an apologetic half smile and tried again. 'I believe he worked in Dunningby?'

Miss Marsh nodded. 'He was learning the hotel business, working his way up from the bottom. I wasn't happy about him being away from Beltour but needs must when the devil drives. It was only temporary, anyhow. A year or two and he'd have got married and settled down here again.'

'I shouldn't have thought there was much scope for a hotelier in Beltour,' ventured MacGregor.

Miss Marsh examined him with cold, hostile eyes. 'Lord Crouch is planning to open a motel on the Claverhouse road. Not that his lordship's affairs are any business of yours.'

'And your nephew was going to get a job there?'

Miss Marsh nodded again. 'He was going to be manager.'

She sighed. 'The best laid plans of mice and men,' she quoted with gloomy relish.

'Do you know if your nephew had any enemies in Dunningby?'

'In Dunningby?' Miss Marsh stared in unflattering astonishment at MacGregor. 'I hope you're not going to waste your time and public money looking for his murderer in Dunningby.'

'You think it was somebody local?'

'I *know* it was somebody local,' said Miss Marsh flatly. 'We've never been accepted in the village, not really. And there are plenty who were jealous of Gary. They've not got a spark of ambition themselves but they just can't bear it when they see somebody else working hard and getting on.'

'Have you anyone particular in mind?'

'No.' Miss Marsh seemed pleased to be so unhelpful. She walked over to the fireplace and straightened one of the wreaths.

MacGregor looked across at Dover to see if he was prepared to shoulder some of the undoubted burden of questioning Miss Marsh but Dover's mind was preoccupied with a more pressing problem. He was calculating the odds of being offered a cup of coffee. They were not good.

MacGregor struggled on. 'I believe your nephew was engaged to be married, Miss Marsh?'

'It was announced officially three weeks ago.'

There was something in the tone of voice with which this statement was made that caused MacGregor to look up sharply. 'You didn't approve?'

Miss Marsh pursed her lips. 'We are told it is better to marry than to burn,' she said. 'And he could have done worse, I suppose. At least the Tiffin girl isn't one of these shameless, fly-by-night little minxes. She's a good bit older than Gary, of course, but she's got her head screwed on and there'll be a bit of money there when Tiffin goes.'

It hardly sounded like the romance of the century and, as

seen through Miss Marsh's jaundiced eyes, Miss Tiffin didn't sound the kind of girl men fight over. MacGregor, however, was in no position to leave any stone unturned. 'Was there, perhaps, some other young man who might have been in love with your nephew's fiancée and . . .?'

Miss Marsh laughed a short, humourless and scornful laugh.

MacGregor waited to see if there was going to be any further comment, but there wasn't. He tried yet another tack. 'Do you think we might just have a look at your nephew's room?'

'Hey, hang on a minute!' Fed up though Dover was with standing there like a lemon, it was still preferable to dashing up and down a lot of blooming stairs. 'Let's hear about what happened over the weekend first.'

Miss Marsh bestowed upon Dover a look which would have come better from a hanging judge. She noted, and condemned, the greasy bowler hat, the even greasier overcoat with its dandruff decorated shoulders, the heavy scuffed black boots. After a short pause to underline her total and absolute disapproval she said, 'Nothing happened over the weekend.'

Dover's face twitched into the blackest of scowls. If there was anything he hated worse than a garrulous witness, it was one who wouldn't talk at all. 'When did he get here?'

'Friday night. He finished too late to catch the train so he had to come round through Claverhouse and catch the bus. He got here about ten.'

'And then?'

Miss Marsh turned away to run her finger along the edge of the table and examine it for dust. 'I gave him his supper and we went to bed.'

Dover's temper was beginning to fray but in the face of Miss Marsh's grim indifference there didn't seem to be much future in blowing his top. 'And Saturday?' he queried through a stiffening jaw.

'Saturday? Well, he did a few jobs for me around the cottage – moving furniture, fetching coal, chopping wood. Then we had lunch. In the afternoon he sat in front of the television watching that sports programme. Then we had tea. After tea he did the washing up for me and then he went over to the Tiffins to watch television at their house.'

MacGregor, seeing that Dover was wilting, chipped in again. 'Did he seem perfectly normal?'

'Yes.'

'He didn't give you any indication that he was in trouble or danger or that he was worried about anything?'

'No.'

'What time did he come home on Saturday night?'

'I'd gone to bed but I heard him come in. It was twenty past eleven. That's ten minutes after Match of the Day ended, so that was about right. The Tiffin's cottage is half a mile from here, just down the road.'

'Sounds as though he had a right lively time,' grumbled Dover.

Miss Marsh had no scruples about putting any man in his place. 'Gary came here for a rest. They worked him very hard in that hotel and he never was one for gadding about. Besides, he was saving up to get married. There was no money for frittering away.'

'All right!' snarled Dover, finally kissing all hopes of a cup of coffee goodbye. 'Sunday?'

'Sunday morning he had a bit of a lie in. Till half past eight. Then he did a few more jobs for me. He washed the windows and oiled the hinges on the kitchen door. After that he got shaved and changed and went to pick up Charmian Tiffin to go to church.'

'Regular church-goer, was he?' asked Dover with a hideous frown. His feet were killing him.

'Not so's you'd notice. I always sent him to Sunday School, of course, when he was little. And he was in the choir for a bit.'

Dover wasn't capable of anything as energetic as pouncing but he did manage to pick Miss Marsh up quite sharply. 'So going to church was something out of the ordinary?'

Miss Marsh was beginning to look bored. She was a woman who liked to keep busy and hanging around here all morning answering stupid and impertinent questions was a waste of her good time. 'Mr Tiffin is the Vicar's Warden. Mrs Tiffin is a pillar of the Mothers' Union – or thinks she is. Even Charmian does a bit of teaching in the Sunday School. Gary was marrying into the family. It made for peace and quiet all round if he toed the line.'

There was a long pause. Neither Miss Marsh nor Dover appeared to have anything further to say. MacGregor waited until the silence had got well beyond the stage of being oppressive and then opened his mouth.

Dover was galvanized into action. 'Shut up, you!' he snapped and swung round on Miss Marsh again. 'Right, that's got us up to going to church on Sunday morning. What happened next?'

'I don't know. I was on duty at Beltour all afternoon and I didn't see him again. He was having his Sunday dinner with the Tiffins and then spending the rest of his time with Charmian. They were engaged, you know. It's only natural that they should want to see something of each other, isn't it?'

'Did you know your nephew was going to see Lord Crouch that evening?' demanded Dover, his eyes narrowing as he tried to look shrewd.

'Of course. There was no secret about it. As a matter of fact Lord Crouch asked me to tell Gary he'd like to see him. And now,' – Miss Marsh moved with determination towards the door – 'if you want to have a look at Gary's room, I'd be obliged if you'd get on with it. I've got things to do. Life has to go on, you know, painful bereavements or no painful bereavements.'

Seven

'I just don't get it!' complained MacGregor as he set a large scotch down in front of Dover. 'Nobody – but nobody – could be that dreary. Not and get themselves murdered.'

'Aaah!' Dover came up for air, smacking his lips. 'That hit the spot all rightie!'

MacGregor shook his head in disbelief. 'I mean, that room of his! Have you ever seen anything, sir, so totally dull and completely lacking in character? All his clothes in neat piles, three or four old school books, a fishing rod and a collection of foreign stamps! That – God help us – was Gary Marsh!'

'Maybe he put all his energy into his sex life,' suggested Dover, upon whom alcohol tended to have a coarsening effect. 'Or maybe he kept all the juicy stuff at this place where he worked.'

MacGregor couldn't help thinking of the time and energy that would be saved if Dover only read the reports from the local police. 'No, there was nothing there either, sir. Inspector Dawkins sent a couple of men round to have a look. Marsh lived in at this hotel and they said his room was about as revealing as a monk's cell.'

'P'raps his auntie cleared away all the incriminating evidence,' said Dover, feeling better as the whisky got to work.

'She said she hadn't touched anything, sir. Just dusted and tidied up a bit. Besides, why should she move anything?'

'She could have croaked him herself.' Dover had taken such a dislike to the inhospitable Miss Marsh that he was even toying with the idea of having her replace Lord Crouch as his chief suspect. 'I wouldn't put anything past that woman.'

'No,' agreed MacGregor, who hadn't cared much for Miss Marsh either. Unlike Dover, though, he wasn't prepared to let personal prejudice cloud his professional judgement. 'On the other hand, sir, there isn't a scrap of evidence of any sort to connect her with the murder.'

'Instinct!' said Dover. 'When you've been a detective as long as me, you develop a nose for these things.'

MacGregor had frequently wondered how Dover reached his more asinine conclusions, and now he knew. However, the knowledge didn't relieve him of the obligation to try and keep Dover's olfactory fancies within reasonable bounds. 'She hasn't any motive, sir,' he pointed out kindly.

Now Dover didn't care for being patronized by anybody, and certainly not by a jumped-up young pouf like MacGregor. 'What about the insurance money?' he snarled.

'The insurance money? But, sir, we don't even know how much it is.'

'Pity you didn't ask, then!' retorted Dover.

'It's probably only a few pounds.'

'I've known murders committed for a few pence,' retorted Dover. It wasn't true but one had to use what weapons one could in the war against MacGregor. 'And I don't reckon there was any love lost between 'em.'

'Well, no, I don't suppose there was, sir, but that doesn't mean ...' MacGregor remembered in time that logical argument didn't cut much ice with Dover and he abandoned it in favour of a simple statement of fact. 'We have no evidence that Miss Marsh was anywhere near the Donkey Bridge or Bluebell Wood at the relevant time on Sunday night, sir.'

'We have no evidence that Miss Marsh was anywhere at all at the relevant time on Sunday night,' Dover yelped in triumph, 'because you, you thick-headed numbskull, didn't bloody well ask her that, either!'

Rebukes are not less galling because they are justified. MacGregor had to admit that he had slipped up but he hoped he was man enough to acknowledge his mistakes when he made them. On the other hand, he would dearly have loved to remind Dover that he, as senior officer, was supposed to be in charge of all aspects of the investigation – and that included the interrogation of witnesses. However, there was no future in drawing Dover's attention to his shortcomings and MacGregor settled for a feeble excuse. 'As a matter of fact, sir,' he said stiffly, 'Miss Marsh was asked to account for her whereabouts during the preliminary investigations by Detective Inspector Dawkins.'

'Oh, your drinking chum!' sneered Dover, who had no difficulty in remembering things when he wanted to be unpleasant. 'Well, bully for him! Well, let's be having it! Where was she? Or are you going to keep that as a little secret just between the two of you?'

'She was at home, sir, in her cottage.'

'Can she prove it?'

'Not really, sir. She was alone.'

'Well, her unsupported word isn't worth a row of pins, is it? Not in my book it bloody well ain't!'

'We shall have to look into it, of course, sir,' agreed MacGregor, though the effort of keeping a civil tongue in his head was well-nigh too much for him. 'Meanwhile, I really do think we ought to see what Miss Tiffin has to say. As his fiancée, she was probably closer to Gary Marsh than anybody and she's bound to know if there was anything going on that might be connected with his murder.' MacGregor, who never learnt, looked hopefully at Dover. 'I was thinking that we could perhaps go along and have a talk with her this afternoon, sir. After you've had your lunch, of course,' he added quickly.

Dover's podgy little nose crinkled up in distaste. 'Strewth, Miss Marsh had been more than enough for one day! He glared balefully at his sergeant. This miserable little bleeder had missed his vocation: he should have been a flipping slave-driver. 'I shall have to have a rest after lunch,' he rumbled. 'That was a nasty fall I had yesterday. And my stomach's been playing me up, too.'

'Perhaps later on, then, sir? I mean, you won't be in bed for the rest of the day, will you?'

Dover's scowl grew darker. 'Tomorrow!' he said firmly. 'What's your sweat? This Tiffin bird's not going to run away.'

'But speed is so important in murder cases, sir,' mumbled MacGregor, unhappily forced to try to instruct his grandmother. 'Especially the first forty-eight hours. If one doesn't get a lead by then. . . . Perhaps if I were to go and see Miss Tiffin?'

'You dare!' Rather than see MacGregor get any credit, Dover would prefer to have Gary Marsh's murderer get away scot free.

The ship's bell, which served The Bull Reborn as a dinner gong, put an end to the discussion and Dover, tossing back the last dregs of his scotch, headed the field in the stampede for the dining room.

After consuming a meal which would have put a lesser man to sleep for good and all, Dover permitted MacGregor to escort him upstairs and into the bedroom. Dover began to remove some of his clothes and MacGregor turned considerately, and squeamishly, away but he was soon brought back to heel.

'Well, don't just stand there!' barked Dover. 'Turn the bloody bed down!'

With a sigh MacGregor obediently pulled off the top cover and then paused in astonishment. 'Goodness, they don't seem to have made the bed very.... Oh, *dear!*'

'What's up?' Dover came staggering across with his trousers at an indelicate half-mast.

The bed clothes had been roughly tugged down, exposing the bottom sheet. And there, in the middle of the bottom sheet, was....

'What is it?' demanded Dover.

MacGregor had already pulled his handkerchief out and clapped it over his nose. The stink!

It took Dover only a second or two longer to get the revolting message. His beady little eyes bulged and his face went an apoplectic purple. 'It's that bloody cat!' he howled. ' 'Strewth, I'll ring its neck for it!' Another outrage caught his attention. 'And look at my pyjamas!' he screamed. 'Look at 'em! They've been torn to bloody shreds!' He reached out a hand quivering with fury and picked up his pyjama jacket to flourish it before MacGregor's gaze. A mangled and long dead mouse rolled out.

It was too much for MacGregor. 'Oh, my God!' he gasped and, stuffing his handkerchief into his mouth, fled the room.

When, some time later, he returned, chalk-faced, he found Dover perched disconsolately on the edge of the sofa.

'Well?'

MacGregor dabbed his lips with his handkerchief and avoided looking either at the bed or at Dover. 'Sir?'

'Haven't you been to fetch the landlord, you lily-livered puke?'

MacGregor opened the window. 'No, sir, I went ...' He flapped a vague hand. 'I'll summon him now, sir.'

The landlord was another person who liked to have his forty winks after lunch but he didn't lose his sense of humour when he was disturbed. 'That damned tom!' he chuckled with frank admiration. 'I don't know how he manages it, honest I don't! You shut all the doors and close all the windows but the cunning little bugger still manages to slip in somehow.'

MacGregor was indignant. 'You mean this has happened before?'

'Dozens of times!' laughed the landlord, wiping away the tears of happy memories with the back of his hand. 'Soon as he gets at outs with one of the guests the old devil's off upstairs making a convenience of the chap's bed before you can say Jack Robinson. And don't think it's a once-and-for-all job, either! Once that cat starts anything, there's no stopping him.'

'Why haven't you drowned the mangy brute?' demanded Dover.

'I can't do that! He's a family pet. Besides, Mr Dover, you can take a joke, can't you? I should have thought you were the sort of bloke who'd appreciate a bit of lavatory humour.'

This appeal to look on the funny side fell on extremely deaf ears and Dover set about cross-examining the landlord with more acuity and ruthlessness than he ever brought to the interrogation of a suspected murderer. It did little good. Mine host stuck to his guns: as an opponent, the ginger cat was implacable and all additional laundry charges would be added to the bill.

'I would offer you the sofa, sir,' said MacGregor, anxious to give the impression of being helpful, 'but it's not very comfortable.'

'He'd track you down there quick as a wink,' boasted the landlord. 'Got a better nose than a bloodhound, that cat!'

'Another room?' asked Dover, without much hope.

'Waste of time,' grinned the landlord. 'Besides, we haven't got one.'

Dover addressed himself to MacGregor. 'Ring up Beltour and tell 'em I'm moving back.'

In normal circumstances MacGregor would have objected very strongly to being landed with such an embarrassing mission but, if it meant getting rid of Dover, he would probably have telephoned Buckingham Palace without a qualm. 'Shall I say you'll be arriving right away, sir?'

Dover gloomily weighed the pros and cons and decided to postpone the evil hour. 'Certainly not!' he snapped. 'I haven't packed in work for the day if you have, laddie! We've got to go and see this Tiffin girl. Tell Lord What's-his-name I'll be there in time for dinner.'

While MacGregor rushed off cheerfully to make all the necessary arrangements, Dover began chucking his belongings back into his suitcase under the amused eye of the landlord. All things considered Dover reckoned Beltour was giving him a pretty raw deal. So raw in fact that it mightn't be a bad idea to clear the murder up in double quick time and catch the first available train back to London. An instant arrest, that was what was needed. Once you'd picked your victim and got him safely tucked away behind bars, you could always fiddle the evidence a bit to make things fit. Dover had done it dozens of times. Of course it didn't always stand up in a court of law but the case wouldn't come up for trial for months and months and by that time anything might have happened. Now, upon whose lucky head should the scales of Justice fall?

The landlord found himself getting a trifle hot round the collar. Dover, who was incapable of doing more than one thing at a time, had stopped packing and was staring unseeingly right through the landlord while he worked out the strategy of getting back to his own bed and his wife's cooking.

The landlord's conscience was pricking him. 'Here, steady on, Mr Dover!' he said with an uneasy laugh. 'You're looking at me as though you were measuring me up for a pair of handcuffs.'

Dover was still trying to decide between Lord Crouch and Miss Marsh. 'Ugh?'

'Oh, come off it!' The landlord managed another unconvincing laugh. 'I'm not so green as I'm cabbage looking, you know. This village idiot act doesn't take me in. It didn't last night and it doesn't now.'

'Eh?' Dover's brow furrowed alarmingly as he gradually became aware that he was in the middle of a conversation.

'It beats me why you couldn't just come straight out and ask me. I'd have told you all about it then, wouldn't I?'

'About what?' asked Dover, looking more moronic than ever.

The landlord was nearly beside himself with exasperation. 'All about me and Gary Marsh, of course! Jesus, you don't half make it hard for a chap! All right, Gary Marsh and me had an argument. I'm not trying to hide it. I was just waiting for you to mention it first that's all. Maybe we both did get a bit worked up and said a bit more than we meant. So what? It's still no reason for you to start looking at me sideways, is it?'

What Dover's response to this well-nigh incoherent statement would have been, the waiting world will never know because it was at precisely this moment that MacGregor came bustling back into the room. His whole future had miraculously assumed a rosy hue and he was as happy as a sandboy. 'All fixed, sir!' he reported with a wide grin. 'Lady Priscilla is delighted to hear that you are returning to Beltour and supper will be at seven.'

'Cold, I suppose,' muttered Dover, steeling himself for the worst.

'Oh, no, sir! Lady Priscilla recognizes that you need building up after your accident and she's going off to the butcher's straight away.'

'The butcher's?' Dover forgot with the utmost ease all about the landlord and his muddled sense of injustice. 'Are we going to have meat?'

'Stewed tripe, sir!' said MacGregor and began finishing off Dover's packing for him. 'There we are, sir! I think that's the lot. Shall we go?'

'Might as well,' grunted Dover as he permitted

MacGregor to help him into his overcoat. 'Where is it we're going?'

'The Tiffins, sir.'

'Oh, yes. Well, come on then!'

'Here, just a minute!' The landlord grasped Dover's arm. 'What about me?'

'You?'

'Holy-Mary-Mother-of-God!' groaned the landlord. 'Don't you want to hear about me and Gary Marsh?'

Dover generously gave him a straight answer to a straight question. 'No,' he said.

Eight

'What was Mr Buckley talking about, sir?' asked MacGregor when he had got Dover comfortably installed in the car.

'Who's Mr Buckley?'

'He's the publican, sir. Of The Bull Reborn. Wasn't he saying something about Gary Marsh?'

Dover grunted. It might have meant anything or – more probably – nothing.

'We'd better have a word with him later, don't you think, sir? He may have some useful information.'

'And pigs might fly,' said Dover, as co-operative and constructive as ever. Still, he didn't want to let MacGregor think that he hadn't got the situation under control. 'I'm letting him stew a bit.'

'Oh,' said MacGregor. He might have been tempted to pursue the matter further if his eye hadn't alighted on the village shop. He opened the car door again. 'Do you mind just hanging on for a second, sir? I've – er – run out of cigarettes.'

Dover gave another of his all purpose grunts and closed his eyes. Many great men have had the priceless ability to drop off to sleep at any time and in any circumstances, and

Chief Inspector Dover was no exception. He was well away by the time MacGregor climbed back into the car and thus missed seeing the little parcel that his sergeant hid with all possible speed in the glove compartment. Even Dover might have thought that it didn't look much like a packet of cigarettes.

MacGregor swung the car out on the road which led to the Beltour estate and grinned to himself. Twenty-seven new pence was a small price to pay for a good night's sleep. That was what the tin of best quality, middle cut salmon had just cost him. He trusted that the ginger cat would enjoy it.

The Tiffins' cottage lay only a few minutes' walk from the big house at Beltour and was mercifully hidden from it by a slight dip in the ground. Originally the cottage must have looked pretty much like the others in the neighbourhood – simple and undistinguished, but pleasing. The Tiffins had changed all that. They had seen the possibilities and had exploited them with a ruthlessness and lack of taste that had to be seen to be believed. No fewer than three coaching lamps (wired for the electric) surrounded the front door and fought it out for *lebensraum* with a particularly rampant Dorothy Perkins. The front door itself sported, on a background of bright yellow, a brass knocker and a brass letter box, a wooden poker-work name plate and a complete set of antique plastic nail heads. Each window had its matching yellow non-functional shutters and in the small front garden a pair of old cart wheels, with each spoke painted a different colour, loomed disproportionately large.

MacGregor shuddered fastidiously and opened the mail-order, wrought iron, bargain offer gate with reluctance. From there he picked his way up the do-it-yourself, crazy paving path and felt grateful that the day was decently overcast. On a bright and sunny afternoon the Tiffins' pad would have been quite unbearable.

Dover, on the other hand, was full of admiration and

envy. He spent a great deal of his time dreaming about his retirement and this was just the sort of place he had in mind. He could just picture himself, snoozing happily in a deck chair in the fresh air and sunshine while his wife dug the garden or chopped the wood. What bliss! As he stood waiting for the front door to be opened, he stared longingly at the sundial and the plaster stork standing next to the little artificial pond. Some people had it with jam on!

'Sir!'

Dover turned round to find the front door open and MacGregor, as befitted a mere underling, standing respectfully to one side. The happy day dreams faded and Dover sighed in an orgy of self pity. Back to the bloody grindstone!

Mrs Tiffin was an admirable match for the cottage, having also been tarted up with more enthusiasm than skill but Dover found her a real queen amongst women. It must be admitted, however, that this realization didn't come to him until he found himself confronted by an afternoon tea of truly heroic proportions. True that, once she was settled presiding over the teapot, Mrs Tiffin turned out to be no mean conversationalist, but with such a feast spread before him Dover was prepared to forgive her even that.

'I made our Charmian go in to work today,' said Mrs Tiffin as she poured out. 'Just to take her mind off things. Well, life has to go on, hasn't it? And it's no good crying over spilt milk. I told her she was doing no good to anybody, moping around the house looking like a wet weekend. She'll be home in about an hour, though, if you want to have a word with her, and her dad comes in about the same time though I don't see that either of them'll be able to tell you anything much. It's a real mystery to us and, believe you me, there's been nothing else discussed in this house since it happened. We've gone on and on about it until I've been fit to scream.'

'It must have been a great shock,' murmured MacGregor.

'I could kill Gary Marsh for getting himself murdered!'

said Mrs Tiffin bitterly. 'I really thought we'd done it this time.'

MacGregor took a polite nibble at his ham sandwich and duly noted the margarine. 'Done it?'

'Got our Charmian settled,' explained Mrs Tiffin, stirring her tea resentfully. 'I warned Arthur what would happen if we buried ourselves down here in the country before we'd got her off our ... before we'd got her nicely settled.'

'Arthur is your husband?'

Mrs Tiffin nodded. 'That's right.'

'So you've not been at Beltour long?'

'A couple of years. We came here just after I'd had my operation.'

'Really?' MacGregor pushed a plate of sausage rolls nearer to Dover. The longer he could keep the old glutton feeding his face, the less likelihood there was of him chipping in and ruining everything.

'The doctors told us I had to take things easy,' Mrs Tiffin went on with the easy complacency of the hypochondriac. 'I'd had a very bad time, you know. Well, the surgeon said he'd never seen anything like it in his life, never. If they hadn't cut me open and taken it out when they did, I wouldn't be sitting here talking to you now.' Mrs Tiffin smiled modestly. 'Touch and go, it was.'

'Fancy,' said MacGregor.

'Of course, up till then, me and Arthur had always worked as a team, you see. He was butler and I did the housekeeping. But, after my operation, they said I had to have a complete rest so Arthur started looking round for a job on his own.'

'You've always been in service, then?' asked MacGregor as he unobtrusively got his notebook out, a feat of *leger-demain* which Dover assisted by shoving his cup across and distracting Mrs Tiffin's attention by imperiously demanding a refill.

'Oh, yes, always.' Mrs Tiffin handed the teacup back and

gave a nervous little start as Dover's other hand shot out like a rapier to grab the last cheese'n'pickle munchie off the plate. 'Mind you, we've always picked our places. We like titled people. They're usually much more considerate and understanding than the merely rich. Oh, well, we did oblige a bishop once, but that was Arthur. He's always been of a very religious turn of mind and his Lordship came from a very good family – unlike some I could name. We did think at one time of trying one of those American millionaires but you never know somehow with foreigners, do you?' Mrs Tiffin filled up the teapot from the hot water jug. 'Mind you, we wouldn't have touched this job here in the normal course of events.'

'No?' MacGregor told himself that you never knew when all these snippets of information might prove valuable.

Mrs Tiffin shook her tightly permed head. 'Well, this is no job for a highly trained, experienced butler like Arthur, is it? It's not a proper butlering job at all. Well, between you and me, I doubt if Lord Crouch and his sister would know what to do with a proper butler if they engaged one. The way they live! Disgusting for titled people, I call it. Pigging it up there in those blooming old box rooms!'

'You can say that again!' growled Dover. He was beginning to show signs of restlessness now that all the food had gone.

MacGregor was quick to recognize the danger signs and he got his cigarette case out. In a couple of seconds he had got Dover sucking away contentedly like a baby. MacGregor returned to Mrs Tiffin. 'What precisely are your husband's duties, Mrs Tiffin?' he asked.

Mrs Tiffin sniffed disparagingly. 'Being a tailor's dummy!' she said. 'He's just there to impress these blooming trippers they have swarming all over the place. Well, he's supposed to sort of keep an eye on things as well. See they don't scratch anything or pinch the cutlery or anything. Oh, and he opens the door to important visitors, too, but mostly he's just there for show. That's why Lord Crouch was so keen on getting

Arthur, you see, because he is such a fine figure of a man. He's got presence, Arthur has. He really looks the part.' Mrs Tiffin smiled contentedly. 'Mind you,' she added, 'I was all against him taking the position.'

'Really?' MacGregor was wondering how and when he was ever going to get Mrs Tiffin down to what some of his detective colleagues liked to call the nitty-gritty stuff. 'Er . . .'

'You can't afford to let your standards slip,' said Mrs Tiffin firmly. 'They soon start taking advantage of you, if they think they can get away with it. Like I said to Arthur at the time, how much ice is a reference from Lord Crouch going to cut? Everybody who is anybody knows the style him and his sister live in. It's all very fine, I said to Arthur, you saying you only did it to oblige but who's going to believe you?'

Who, indeed? MacGregor smiled the uncertain smile of one who is hopelessly lost.

Mrs Tiffin took pity on him. 'Arthur was Lord Crouch's batman,' she explained. 'Donkey's years ago now, of course. Well, you'd think that was grounds for Lord Crouch doing Arthur a good turn, wouldn't you, instead of the other way round? What's got into you? I said to Arthur. You've never so much as mentioned your Army service these past twenty years and now here you are taking a stupid position like this on the strength of it. Well, he mumbled something about the money being very good. Just like a man. And then there's our Charmian to think of, I told him.'

'Oh, yes,' said MacGregor feebly.

'I wasn't a bit keen on coming down here to the back of beyond because of her. I mean, whichever way you look at it, a girl has more chances in London than she does in the country. It stands to reason, doesn't it? Oh, I know Gary turned up here in Beltour but that still doesn't alter the principle of the thing. Arthur was like a dog with two tails when they announced their engagement but, don't count your chickens, I said. There's many a slip, I said. And I was right! Our Charmian's worse off now than if she'd never met the dratted boy!'

'Ah, yes, Gary Marsh!' MacGregor stole a glance at Dover and tried to calculate how much longer Mrs Tiffin's substantial tea was going to keep him pinned down in his chair. The time for ruthlessness had come and MacGregor cut through Mrs Tiffin's bitter maternal lamentations over the loss of a prospective son-in-law. 'I believe Gary Marsh spent most of the day he was killed here, Mrs Tiffin?'

Mrs Tiffin agreed sadly that he had. 'And I was so looking forward to it, too,' she complained. 'You see, Gary didn't often get a weekend off and, when he came home in the middle of the week, our Charmian was at work. I thought this weekend was going to be a wonderful opportunity for us all to get to know one another better.'

'You didn't know Gary Marsh well, then?'

'Not really. Well, until our Charmian started going out with him a month or so ago, I don't even remember so much as seeing him. I must have done, I suppose, but he just didn't register somehow.'

MacGregor felt he could understand that. 'Did you or Mr Tiffin have any objections to the engagement?'

'Good heavens, no! Gary was a very nice boy ... really. Once you got to know him. And, of course, anything Charmian wanted was all right by her father and me. She's our only child, you know, so I suppose we do tend to spoil her a bit. Still, she's a very sensible girl and we do want to see her settled. She's had one or two disappointments in the past, you know, and we did so hope everything was going to work out this time.'

'Perhaps you could tell me exactly what happened on Sunday,' said MacGregor, earning top marks for dogged determination. 'Did Gary seem perfectly normal?'

'Well,' – Mrs Tiffin paused as she gave her answer some thought – 'he hadn't much to say for himself but, then, I think he was probably always a bit like that. You'd have to ask our Charmian.' Mrs Tiffin looked coy. 'She's the one who'd know whether he was his usual self or not.'

'What did you do on Sunday?'

'Do? Well,' – Mrs Tiffin sat back with a sigh – 'I don't know that we actually *did* anything. Charmian and her dad went to church and Gary met them there. I gave it a miss that morning because I had to see to the dinner. I wanted it to be something a bit special. Well, after church Arthur and Gary went to The Bull Reborn for a drink and Charmian came straight back here to give me a hand. Then we had dinner and, after dinner, Charmian and Gary watched television in here. Arthur came and gave me a hand with the washing up and then we just sort of generally kept out of the way. Well, you do, don't you? Round about five o'clock I got the tea ready and took it in. By the time we'd finished that it was time for Gary to leave. I did suggest that Charmian might like to walk over with Gary to Beltour and maybe even wait while he saw Lord Crouch and then go to the station with him, but her dad wouldn't hear of it. Mind you, it was coming on to rain but she could have taken her mac. Arthur said he wasn't having her come all that way back from the station by herself in the dark. In view of what happened to poor Gary, I suppose he was right but I wasn't too pleased with him at the time, I don't mind telling you. Well, you know what young couples are like and a nice walk through the woods can be so romantic, can't it?'

MacGregor was scribbling away like a maniac, much to Dover's sardonic and sleepy amusement, but the sergeant was keeping a firm grip on the essentials. 'Just a minute, Mrs Tiffin! You knew that Gary Marsh was going to see Lord Crouch that evening?'

'Oh, yes. Gary mentioned it at dinner.'

'And you knew he would be walking from Beltour House, through Bluebell Wood and across the Donkey Bridge to the railway station?'

'Yes.'

'He told you that, too?'

Mrs Tiffin wrinkled her brow. 'Well, no, not in so many words, I suppose. I just assumed that's what he'd do. I mean, if you're walking, it's the obvious way, isn't it? Miles quicker than going round by the road.' She glanced up at the clock on the mantelpiece. 'Good heavens, is that the time? Well, if you want to ask me any more questions, you'll just have to wait a bit. I've got to get Arthur's tea ready for him. He likes to have it as soon as he gets in. Would either of you two gentlemen like another cup?'

Dover heard that all right. 'Yes,' he said and yawned noisily as he watched Mrs Tiffin begin to pile up the empty plates. 'Here,' he said, generous to a fault, 'my sergeant'll give you a hand with that. Come on, MacGregor! Where's your manners?' Dover gave Mrs Tiffin a conspiratorial wink. 'You play your cards properly, missus, and he might even wash up for you! He's very domesticated. Make some girl a first-rate husband!'

Mrs Tiffin examined MacGregor with renewed interest. 'He's not married, then?' she asked with a little laugh, as though it was all some big joke.

'An unplucked rose!' Dover assured her maliciously.

'Fancy!' Mrs Tiffin subjected MacGregor to another shrewd going over. 'Er – are you likely to be staying in the district for long?'

Dover dragged his chair nearer to the fire as MacGregor banged crossly out into the kitchen with the load of plates a beaming Mrs Tiffin had handed him. 'No idea,' said Dover. 'Sometimes these cases take days to clear up, sometimes weeks.'

'Weeks?' echoed Mrs Tiffin thoughtfully. 'Fancy! Well, I just hope you'll look upon this house as your second home while you're here. Pop in any time you feel like a drink or a meal. We'll always be very glad to see you. Both of you, of course.'

'I'll remember that!' promised Dover with a smirk.

MacGregor came back from the kitchen only to receive another armful of plates from a now gushing Mrs Tiffin. 'Come on!' she exhorted him gaily. 'I'll wash and you can wipe. All right, dear?'

Nine

When MacGregor eventually returned to the sitting room, he had a face like thunder. Grimly he rolled his shirt sleeves down and put his jacket on. Dover, feeling the draught, opened one eye.

'That, sir,' said MacGregor in a voice which he failed to keep steady, 'was not very funny.'

Dover opened the other eye. 'What wasn't?'

MacGregor ignored the question and stalked away across the room to sit down as far from Dover as he could get. He reached for his notebook and began ruffling through the pages in an effort to still his beating heart. 'She's been telling me what a good cook her daughter is!' he whined.

Dover rearranged several pounds of fat more comfortably in his chair. 'She probably thinks you're quite a good catch,' he grunted. 'Sprightly young bachelor with a steady job and a pension at the end of it.'

'Well, I think it's positively indecent! Her daughter's fiancée isn't in his grave yet, poor devil, and that woman's already looking round for a replacement.'

Dover felt a faint twinge of sympathy but he managed to suppress it before it showed. He had been snared by a designing mother himself and was still nursing the grudge. Baiting MacGregor, though, was always an enjoyable exercise. 'You could probably do worse,' he observed, endeavouring to sound like a Dutch uncle. 'It's about time you settled down and shouldered your responsibilities like the rest of us.'

But MacGregor was not to be drawn. 'There's a man,' he said, looking out of the window by which he was sitting. 'He's just coming through the garden gate. Pushing a bicycle.'

It was Arthur Tiffin, looking less impressive now that he had exchanged his butler's outfit for a pair of grey flannel trousers and a sports coat. Dover found him almost as charming as Mrs Tiffin. And equally generous, as witness his prompt offer to share his high tea with the strangers at his gates. There was, he remarked good-naturedly, more than enough ham and eggs in the dish for them all. Dover, helping himself first, promptly proved him wrong.

In between the sparse mouthfuls that still remained to him, Mr Tiffin revealed that the death of Gary Marsh had been a deep personal tragedy. 'On account of our little Charmian,' he explained and MacGregor leaned forward in an attempt to catch his sorrowful words over the noise of Dover's guzzling. 'If she was one of these flashy young bits you see all over the place, I wouldn't worry so much,' Mr Tiffin went on miserably, 'but she's not. She's sort of a bit shy and retiring and it takes time to get to know her.'

'We should have stayed in London,' said Mrs Tiffin, who was once again presiding over the teapot. 'She'd more choice there. We should have stayed.'

It was obviously a well-chewed bone of domestic contention and Mr Tiffin set aside his grief to make the rejoinders which he had no doubt made a hundred times before. 'We lived in London for years and much good it did her.'

'There was that chauffeur with those Peruvians!' snapped

Mrs Tiffin, blinking as Dover reached right across her to get at the bread and butter.

'Did a moonlight flit,' explained Mr Tiffin in a disgruntled aside to MacGregor. 'Two blooming days after I'd footed the bill for their engagement party.'

Mrs Tiffin glared at her husband. 'And who was it who told him she was anaemic? Honestly, Arthur, you've put more spokes in that girl's wheel over your dratted glasses of beer than . . .'

'I've got to have a chat with them!' protested Mr Tiffin. 'I'm her father. I can't let her get tied up with some man we know nothing about.'

'There's chats and chats,' grumbled Mrs Tiffin. 'And we know which sort yours are! What about that nice young school teacher in Chelsea that she met at those art appreciation classes?'

'They sent him to prison for interfering with little boys! That was nothing to do with me!'

'It only happened after you'd had a heart-to-heart talk with him in The Golden Cross.'

'Well, damn it all, woman,' – Mr Tiffin mopped up the last vestiges of his fried egg with a piece of bread – 'I did find out that he'd already got a wife, didn't I?'

Mrs Tiffin regarded her spouse sourly. 'Sometimes, Arthur,' she said, 'I wonder whether, deep down, you really want to see our Charmian get married.'

'Of course I want her to get married!' Mr Tiffin glanced at MacGregor and risked a resigned shrug of his shoulders. 'I want it as much as you do.'

'Then why don't you leave things alone?' demanded Mrs Tiffin. 'You've always got to go poking your nose in, you have. Look what you've done to Gary!'

The unfortunate Mr Tiffin cringed and looked anxiously at his two guests. 'Here, steady on, love!' he pleaded. 'You'll be getting me into trouble, saying silly things like that. It's not my fault Gary got murdered.'

'He was perfectly all right until you took him off for a drink and another of your precious man-to-man talks!' retorted his wife, clearly intent upon having the last word if it killed her.

Dover was now down to his last spoonful of sherry trifle and MacGregor realized that he was in danger of wasting his opportunities. He broke through the matrimonial in-fighting. 'Ah, yes, Mr Tiffin! Now, you took Gary Marsh to The Bull Reborn for a drink after church, didn't you?'

Mr Tiffin, who had been successfully harried into thinking that every man's hand was against him, was instantly on the defensive. 'And what's wrong with that?' he demanded heatedly. 'There's nothing incompatible in being a church warden and having a drink, is there? You don't have to sign the pledge to be a member of the Church of England, you know.'

'Well, no,' agreed MacGregor, rather taken aback. 'I never said you ...'

'More often than not, you'll find the Vicar himself in there, enjoying a quiet pint after Matins. You go to the Noncomformists, sergeant, if you want total abstinence! Alcohol is as much the gift of God as anything else and, as long as it's used in moderation ...'

'Oh, quite!' said MacGregor hastily. 'I couldn't agree with you more, actually. But it's Gary Marsh I'm really interested in.'

'He had a lemonade shandy,' said Mr Tiffin, unmollified.

MacGregor was not surprised. From what he had gathered about the late Gary Marsh, a lemonade shandy would appear to be just about his mark.

Dover, inevitably, sparked into life again. He pushed his chair back from the table and smacked his lips. A glass of beer would go down a fair treat just now.

Unfortunately, Mr Tiffin was fully occupied with answering MacGregor's questions. 'Did he seem worried?' Mr Tiffin hunched his shoulders. 'Well, it's hard to tell. Gary wasn't the sort of lad who wore his heart on his sleeve. To tell you the truth, I could hardly get a word out of him.'

The irrepressible Mrs Tiffin chipped in again. 'That's probably because you were doing all the talking,' she said. 'As usual. Well, somebody must have said something because you both turned up here for your dinners with faces as long as fiddles. I made sure something had gone wrong … again.'

'And I told you you were mistaken, didn't I?' Mr Tiffin stared resentfully at his wife. 'You know your trouble, don't you? You imagine things.'

Dover's patience was becoming exhausted. He roused himself to take a guiding hand in the conversation. 'While you were having a *drink* together,' he said, carefully emphasizing and clearly ennunciating the relevant word, 'what did you talk about?'

It was too subtle for Mr Tiffin. 'Oh, this and that,' he said vaguely.

The sullen scowl which crossed over Dover's face indicated, even to the most obtuse, that this answer was not satisfactory.

Mr Tiffin tried again. 'The lad's prospects, you know. After all, he was proposing to marry our only child and I naturally wanted to know how he envisaged his future.'

'You were supposed to be making a few enquiries about his past!' That was Mrs Tiffin, displaying the infallible memory which wives of her calibre always seem to possess. 'We knew his future was secure, what with Lord Crouch taking such an interest in him. It was his past I wanted clearing up.'

Mr Tiffin poured some milk into his cup and irritably tossed in a couple of lumps of sugar. 'Oh, good grief, Alice, nobody bothers about that sort of thing these days.'

'Oh, don't they?' sniffed Mrs Tiffin, resolutely folding her arms and forcing her husband to stretch for the teapot himself. 'Well, that's a nice thing for a religious man like you to say!'

Mr Tiffin ground his teeth and turned the other cheek.

Mrs Tiffin smacked that, too. 'Of course, I happen to care about my daughter's future happiness. I'd nothing against poor Gary, really, but there was a mystery about his birth and you were supposed to be getting to the bottom of it.'

'Gossip,' muttered Mr Tiffin as he watched a thin dribble of tea struggle out of the pot and quarter fill his cup. 'Idle gossip.'

'Gossip it may be,' agreed Mrs Tiffin with the triumphant air of one about to score the winning point. 'But idle it certainly wasn't. Why, there's hardly a soul in this village that hasn't been credited with fathering or mothering that boy at one time or another. Up to and including Lord Crouch.'

'I told you I asked Gary all about it,' said Mr Tiffin dispiritedly. 'And you want to be careful what you say about his lordship. There's such a thing as slander.'

The Tiffins were obviously squaring up for the next round and MacGregor sensed that it might well be now or never. He took full advantage of Mrs Tiffin's slight hesitation as she mulled over the prospects of being sued by Lord Crouch for defamation of character. 'Ah, yes! Gary Marsh's antecedents! You discussed them with him, Mr Tiffin?'

'Oh, no! Not you, too!' Mr Tiffin was clearly distressed to find that the police were allying themselves with his wife. 'Good grief, anybody would think we'd still got Queen Victoria on the throne! Look, Gary Marsh was illegitimate. So what? It was hardly his fault, was it? And, in spite of what some of the clever devils in this village may say, there's no mystery about his parentage. His mother was Miss Marsh's younger sister and his father was some passing commercial traveller or sailor or something. I don't know and I doubt very much if his mother did, either. She was that sort of girl. Before Gary was six months old she cleared off again with some new gentleman friend and, apart from a couple of postcards, that's the last anybody's heard of her. She's not going to come around bothering anybody now.'

MacGregor studiously wrote all this down and Dover continued to watch him with sardonic contempt. It was widely believed up at Scotland Yard that the chief inspector couldn't even sign his own name, but this was a vile calumny on a scholar who had left more than one indelible mark in the outside lavatories of Mafeking Street Boys' School. MacGregor looked up from his notebook but Mrs Tiffin was already stirring it up again.

'A likely story!' she scoffed. 'So how do you explain all the interest Lord Crouch was taking in him? He practically reared that lad as his own, by all accounts.'

'He did nothing of the sort!' snapped Mr Tiffin.

'He did! Everybody says so!'

'He didn't! And they don't!'

'You know your trouble, don't you, Arthur Tiffin?' Mrs Tiffin's rhetorical question was withering. 'You're soft! You believe anything anybody tells you.'

It was a harsh accusation to make about a man of Mr Tiffin's social standing but Mrs Tiffin was a bitterly disappointed woman. Fate had robbed her (and not for the first time) of a mate for her daughter but Fate was not available for reproach and retaliation. Mr Tiffin, on the other hand, was.

Before very long Mr Tiffin took the coward's way out.

'Where are you going?' demanded his ever-loving.

Mr Tiffin smiled a rather silly smile. 'Just upstairs, dear. I shan't be a minute.'

'Typical!' snorted Mrs Tiffin as soon as her husband had left the room. 'He does it on purpose,' she told Dover. 'Every time. Regular as clockwork. Soon as he starts losing an argument – off to the bathroom. Claims he's got a weak bladder. The result of his army service, so he says. If you ask me, it's a weak head he's suffering from, not a weak bladder.'

And so, when Mr Tiffin returned from his little expedition, the bickering continued. Dover, surprisingly, didn't seem to mind though he was not usually noted for his tolerance of witnesses who couldn't give a straight answer to a blunt question. Today, however, he was prepared to play a waiting game. According to his calculations Miss Tiffin should be arriving on the scene at any moment and with her – with any luck – his third high tea of the afternoon.

At least when Miss Tiffin did turn up, it put an end to the domestic brawling. The decencies had to be preserved in the face of such a cruel loss. In a hushed voice Mrs Tiffin urged her daughter to try and eat something but Miss Tiffin, red-eyed and snively, was not to be persuaded. Dover took an instant dislike to the girl.

Charmian Tiffin was a girl only by courtesy, of course. She was actually twenty-nine, claimed to be twenty-six and looked a good forty. As MacGregor examined her sharp, sallow features, her mousy hair and her generally lethargic bearing, he could only conclude that she would have made a fitting partner for the deceased and dreary Gary Marsh. The only puzzle was how two such utterly negative characters had ever got to the stage of plighting their troths in the first place. MacGregor guessed that Mrs Tiffin might have quite a lot to answer for.

The introductions were made and Miss Tiffin indicated to the accompaniment of some half-hearted grizzling and a tentative dab at her eyes with an already sodden handkerchief that she was willing to undergo the ordeal of being questioned. Dover's face slipped back into its discontented scowl and MacGregor turned to a fresh page in his notebook. But Mrs Tiffin, a devoted mother if ever there was one, had other ideas. On the painfully thin pretext of getting her daughter to take a dose of iron tonic, she inveigled the girl into the kitchen and there, presumably, gave her a rapid run down on the facts of life. A considerably more animated Miss Tiffin duly returned to the sitting room and joined MacGregor on the settee. The sergeant who, in his innocence, had imagined that Mrs Tiffin and her daughter had merely been plotting to pervert the ends of justice, found himself breaking out in a cold sweat. Miss Tiffin edged a couple of inches closer and managed a watery smile.

Dover now found himself in something of a predicament and he was obliged to make his mind up quickly as to which he disliked the more: Charmian Tiffin or his sergeant. Miss Tiffin won the unpopularity contest by a short head because, much as Dover relished MacGregor's embarrassment, there wasn't much joy sitting in a house where no more food was going to be served. The only thing to do now was to get out as quickly as possible and so, with this end firmly in mind, Dover silenced MacGregor with a warning scowl and took over the interrogation himself.

'I suppose you know,' he began, just to put the girl at her ease, 'that you're my principle suspect in this murder case?'

It was news to Miss Tiffin and she stopped ogling MacGregor with gratifying abruptness. It was a surprise to her doting parents, too, and after a moment's shocked silence the storm of outraged protests broke.

Dover talked through them. 'In my experience,' he bawled, 'people always get themselves snuffed out by their nearest and dearest. One of the laws of nature. And if you lot,' he added venomously, addressing the family group en bloc, 'don't keep your blooming traps shut, I'll take little Miss Weeping Willow here down to the nick and question her there. Without witnesses!'

Since this dire threat was accompanied by some pretty daunting muscle flexing on Dover's part, the Tiffins's expostulations spluttered away into an apprehensive silence.

'That's better!' said Dover, nodding his head with great satisfaction before singling out Miss Tiffin again for his undivided attention. 'So, it's up to you, girl, isn't it? You play ball with me and I'll play ball with you. Get it?'

'But I didn't do it!' moaned Miss Tiffin, wringing her hands.

'Of course, she didn't!' screamed her mother.

Dover spared a moment to deal with this outburst of parental concern. 'Button it!' he advised.

Mrs Tiffin rose to her feet. 'Arthur,' she demanded hysterically, 'are you going to sit there and let me be spoken to like that?'

'He will if he's any sense!' chuckled Dover, beginning quite to enjoy himself. 'I'll run him in as an accessory, else! You, too, if I hear another squawk out of you!' And having successfully bitten the hands that had fed him, Dover turned back to Miss Tiffin. 'Well, made your mind up yet?'

'But I told you,' whimpered Miss Tiffin, 'I didn't do it!'

Dover assumed an expression more of anger than of sorrow. 'Oh, well, if you want to play it the hard way . . .'

'I couldn't have done it!' whined Miss Tiffin. 'I was with Mumsy all evening. Right from the time Gary left to go and see Lord Crouch until Daddy came in after the evening service. Then I was with both of them until we went to bed. I've got an alibi.'

'Call that an alibi!' jeered Dover. ' 'Strewth, I've seen better alibis crawling out of mouldy cheese. It isn't worth the paper it's written on. You'll have to do better than that, girl!'

'I loved Gary! I was going to marry him!'

'Practically putting the noose round her own neck,' commented Dover to Mr Tiffin in an amiable aside. 'Best motive I've heard for a month of Sundays.'

'Oh, you brute!' sobbed Miss Tiffin.

'What was he going to see Lord Crouch for anyhow?'

'I don't know. Something to do with business, I expect. Gary' – Miss Tiffin's sobs doubled as she remembered all she had lost – 'Gary didn't believe in women worrying their heads about business so, of course, I didn't ask.'

'Shows the lad had some sense,' grunted Dover who prided himself on being very much of a Kinder, Kirche, Kuche man.

MacGregor, suspecting that Mrs Tiffin might be about to nail the flag of Women's Lib to her masthead and so confuse what little issue there was, intervened smoothly in an attempt to cool things down. 'Perhaps they were discussing this new motel that Lord Crouch is going to open?' he suggested. 'I believe that your late fiancé was going to manage it?'

Miss Tiffin nodded and gave MacGregor such a grateful smile that he regretted that he hadn't left her to Dover's tender mercies.

But, even for the handsome and eligible sergeant, Mrs Tiffin was not prepared to bottle up her righteous wrath for long. 'Now, just you look here!' she all but shouted at Dover. 'Our Charmian had nothing to do with Gary's death, and neither did I, and neither did her dad! I don't know what sort of a game you think you're playing but, if you ask me, things have gone just about far enough. I'm not trying to teach you your job but, if this is the way Scotland Yard investigates a murder, the sooner something is done about it the better. You're nothing but a great bully! Arthur,' – she gave her husband a commanding nod – 'just give your friend, the Chief Constable, a ring! And' – she swung back to Dover again – 'if he can't do anything, we shall have to have a word with Lord Crouch. Luckily the Home Secretary is a cousin of his, by marriage.'

Dover sunk back in his chair. If there was one thing that riled him more than another, it was having a bloody woman shouting at him. Especially one with connections. In his chequered career Dover had had too many complaints brought against him not to know the grief and unpleasantness they brought in their wake. It just wasn't worth the trouble, to say nothing of the fact that one more blot on the Dover escutcheon would probably lead to instant and ignominious dismissal. Dover reckoned he'd better not chance his arm. He scowled at Mrs Tiffin. 'Oh, all right!' he muttered sullenly. 'Have it your way! No need to fly off the bloody handle!' He heaved himself up a little in his chair. 'By the way,' he asked, 'who do you think did it?'

Ten

'Very tricky case,' said Dover. 'Endless complications and ramifications. Not,' he added complacently, just in case anybody should have any doubts, 'that I haven't cracked plenty worse in my time.'

His companions at the dinner table, Lord Crouch and Lady Priscilla, stared fascinated at the oracle. So this was how Scotland Yard really worked! It was quite incredible!

Dover basked happily in the atmosphere of awed attention and obligingly launched into some highly coloured and totally fictitious reminiscences. Sinister Chinese, criminal master-minds, blood-thirsty gangsters and cunning psychopaths flitted across the scene, only to find themselves being cut down in their evil prime through the personal courage and rapier sharp mind of the speaker.

Lord Crouch and Lady Priscilla were dumb-struck.

All in all, Dover's return to Beltour had been highly successful. He had arrived in nice time for supper and nobody had been so ill-bred as to mention either his peculiar withdrawal to The Bull Reborn or his even more peculiar return from it. The stewed tripe, specially prepared by Lady Priscilla's noble hands, hardly reached the standards

Dover usually required in either quality or quantity but, for once, even this didn't matter as Dover's stomach was still trying to cope with the blow-out it had received in the Tiffins' cottage. Indeed, so strained were Dover's digestive processes that he was obliged to bestow upon his hosts the supreme accolade of undoing the top button of his trousers before tackling the tinned treacle pudding which Lady Priscilla had bought for him, 2p off.

Lady Priscilla smiled happily. Nothing that Dover did either surprised or shocked her. To her he was a real man of the people, a son of the soil, and if his ways were not as hers she knew she was in no position to criticize. 'How absolutely fascinating!' she breathed as Dover brought his lurid account of how he had bust up gangland single-handed to a close.

A lump of pudding slowly dropped off one of Dover's chins and sank without a trace in the rest of the debris on his waistcoat.

'What interesting lives you ordinary people lead!' cooed Lady Priscilla enviously. 'It's been a revelation, it really has. Watching you at work, I mean. I just didn't realize how you had to go about things. Silly old me, I thought you spent all your time searching for clues!' She chuckled indulgently at her own stupidity. 'You know, examining the scene of the crime with a magnifying glass and analysing bloodstains and measuring footprints and everything.'

For one dreadful moment Dover thought that Lady Priscilla was taking the mickey. When he realized that she wasn't, however, he relaxed and even consented to explain his peculiar technique. 'I use the psychological approach,' he said modestly. 'Brains, that's my speciality!' Solemnly he tapped the side of his head with a grubby, nicotine stained finger.

Lady Priscilla nodded with complete understanding. 'Of course!' she agreed eagerly. 'You know my trouble, Mr Dover! I read too many of those dreadful detective stories!

They're just too fantastic, aren't they? I mean, one couldn't expect people to go rushing around like that in real life, could one?'

Dover bestirred himself to put the record straight. 'I've hardly been letting the grass grow under my feet!' he pointed out truculently.

'No, no, of course not!' Lady Priscilla hastened to placate Dover before he could turn nasty. 'Besides, I expect you leave all that routine stuff to your sergeant. Such a nicely spoken, well mannered boy, I thought.'

She could have been more tactful. Dover's face broke into a discontented scowl. 'That bloody young pansy?' he snarled. 'Believe you me, missus, I'd be sitting pretty if I didn't have that snivelling little queer tied round my neck twenty-four hours a day!'

Lady Priscilla belonged to a generation which was not accustomed to having the sexual proclivities of third parties discussed, however obliquely and unfoundedly, at the dinner table. She went slightly pink and changed the conversation. 'Er – are you going out again tonight, chief inspector?'

Dover looked highly aggrieved. ' 'Strewth,' he groaned, 'I'm not made of flipping iron!'

It took Lady Priscilla a second or two to work out that the answer to her perfectly straightforward question was in the negative. 'Oh, well, in that case,' – she turned brightly to her brother – 'I think we might offer Mr Dover a glass of port, don't you, Boys?'

Lord Crouch inclined his head and rose from the table with all the ponderous dignity, if not the speed, of a Saturn rocket at take-off.

Lady Priscilla went on chatting to Dover. 'My dear father was something of a connoisseur where wine was concerned, you know, though it was our grandfather, of course, who laid down the cellar. He had quite a reputation, I believe, for shrewd buying and of course he had the very best advice from his shippers.'

The prospect of getting his paws on the cream of Beltour's wine cellar quite brought out Dover's sunnyside again and, sweeping his pudding plate out of the way, he cleared the decks eagerly for action. His brief sojourn at The Bull Reborn had obviously inspired his hosts to spark up their ideas a bit. They'd finally learned that a stalwart, red-blooded fellow like Dover needed more than this teetotal, vegetarian pap to keep him happy. Dover licked his lips. Vintage port as laid down by old grandpa, eh? A couple of bottles of that and he'd sleep the sleep of the just!

Lord Crouch ambled back from the kitchen with a bottle in his hand. Unlike the late earl, Dover hardly ranked as a connoisseur in anything more exotic than bottled beer, but even he could read.

Lady Priscilla sensed that somehow she had raised Dover's hopes a deal too high. 'Of course,' she explained as her brother methodically opened the bottle of invalid tonic wine, 'what was left of the cellar was sold off years ago. Death duties, you know. However, they recommended this label very highly in the village shop. With Boys and myself not' – she gave an apologetic little laugh – 'indulging, we are obliged to lean rather heavily upon the opinions of the experts. I do hope you'll find it agreeable to your palate.'

The sullen quivering of Dover's jowl should have been enough to indicate his opinion to anyone, but Lady Priscilla was in many ways one of Nature's innocents and, as she watched glassful after glassful slurp down Dover's throat, she simply assumed that he must be enjoying the stuff. She was wrong. Dover was drinking this invalid muck because there was no hope of getting anything else, but it was not quenching his thirst for vengeance.

Judging that Lord Crouch was probably even more of a jellyfish than his sister, Dover directed his gimlet eye – as yet unaffected by the booze – on that unfortunate nobleman.

'You got an alibi for What's-his-name's murder?' he

demanded while coming up for air after a particularly lengthy guzzle.

'I beg your pardon?' spluttered Lord Crouch, stung for once in his life into a fairly prompt verbal reaction.

Dover reached for the bottle. 'I've fancied you right from the start,' he observed conversationally. 'The way I look at it, you've got the lot. Means, motive, opportunity. You're tailor-made for it.'

'Good heavens!' Lady Priscilla stared in astonishment at her brother before turning to stare in even greater astonishment at Dover. 'Boys?'

'He even looks guilty,' grunted Dover.

This was quite true. Lord Crouch's nervous system had finally conveyed the full implication of Dover's remarks to his brain and his lordship's face had gone a brick and painful red.

'Oh, 'strewth, come on!' urged Dover irritably. 'Say something if it's only goodbye!'

Lord Crouch did try but, before he was anywhere near actually getting anything out, Lady Priscilla had plunged headlong into the breach. She had a highly developed protective instinct where her brother was concerned. She knew his limitations and she wasn't going to stand by and see him bullied, even by a member of the working class. 'He didn't do it!' she said firmly.

'Tell me the old, old story!' chanted Dover, getting boisterous as the tonic wine began coursing through his veins.

'Left here a'right!' gasped Lord Crouch, making a supreme effort.

'You see?' Lady Priscilla smiled encouragingly at her brother. 'Gary Marsh was perfectly all right when he left here.'

'Well, of course he blooming well was!' snorted Dover. 'Nobody's arguing the toss about that, are they? It's what happened after he left that matters. When him and His Nibs here took that last fatal walk together to the railway station.'

'But they didn't!' protested Lady Priscilla, not even waiting for the denial that was attempting to force its way out of Lord Crouch's throat. 'Gary was alone when he left Beltour.'

Dover showed the generous side of his nature. 'Prove it!'

Lady Priscilla hesitated. 'But we don't have to, do we?' she questioned doubtfully. 'I thought the police were the ones who had to prove things.'

Dover had no intention of getting involved in a discussion on the workings of British Justice at that time of night. 'What clothes was he wearing on Sunday evening?'

Lady Priscilla was nimble-witted only in comparison with her brother. 'Clothes?'

'Assuming he didn't conduct his interview with Who's-your-father stark naked, he must have worn some clothes, mustn't he? Right, let's have a look at 'em! One spot of mud and I'll clap the bracelets on him here and now.' Dover, flushed with invalid port, was beginning to enjoy himself. It wasn't often that he got the opportunity of giving a couple of your blue-blooded aristocrats the old run around.

Lady Priscilla was consulting her brother. 'You were wearing your grey suit on Sunday, weren't you, dear?'

Lord Crouch managed a confirmatory nod of his head.

'I took it to the cleaners on Monday morning!' whispered Lady Priscilla, her face going white.

Dover chuckled in a particularly nauseating way. 'What about his boots?'

'His boots?' Lady Priscilla clutched her heart. 'I always clean Boys' shoes for him first thing in the morning, before breakfast. The public expect him to look wellgroomed, you see, and he's so absent-minded that if I don't ...' She realized that her voice was degenerating into a panicky gabble so she stopped herself and concentrated on a simple statement of the vital fact. 'There was absolutely no mud on them. That I swear.'

'And a fat lot of good it'll do you!' sniffed Dover,

fortifying himself with another draught of his elixir. 'We'll see what the lab's got to say about it.'

Lady Priscilla rose from the dinner table with touching natural dignity. There might have been a tumbril waiting outside the door. 'I will get the shoes for you immediately,' she announced. 'My brother and I have nothing to fear.'

It would have been a more impressive declaration if the sound of Lord Crouch's teeth chattering had not been so loud.

A few seconds later Dover found himself clutching a pair of very large, hand-made, brown shoes which had been dumped, with praiseworthy restraint, in his lap. More was to follow. On the table in front of him, Lady Priscilla laid a small piece of paper.

'That,' she said in a voice dripping with icicles, 'is the ticket for Boys's grey suit. You can enquire at the cleaner's if there was any mud on it.'

Dover's podgy face creased in dismay. God only knows, he'd enough work already on his plate without ... 'Strewth, couldn't people take a joke? He downed the last dregs of his invalid wine and tried to stuff the shoes out of sight under the table. 'I reckon it's about time I was turning in,' he muttered. 'I've had a hard day, you know, and' – he made one of his revolting bids for sympathy – 'I'm not feeling at all well.'

'Don't you wish to ask my brother any further questions?'

Dover was now intent only on sliding out from under. He tried a conciliatory tone. 'Nothing that can't wait till morning. He can make a statement to my sergeant.'

'I would prefer to have this business settled tonight,' said Lady Priscilla, the bit now firmly between her teeth. 'Boys won't be able to sleep a wink if he goes to bed with all these vague accusations hanging over him. And neither shall I. It doesn't matter to us if it takes all night.'

It mattered to Dover but, in the increasingly chilly

circumstances, he thought it wiser not to say so. He'd just have to go through the motions and ask a few damn fool questions otherwise, he could tell from the look on Lady Priscilla's face, there'd be ructions. The trouble was – and here Dover stirred up the dandruff as he scratched his head disconsolately – he couldn't for the life of him think of any blasted questions to ask.

Lady Priscilla unwittingly gave him a few more moments grace. 'You'll need a pencil and some paper,' she announced, and went off in search of them.

Lord Crouch and Dover eyed each other in mutual apprehension. Eventually, after a certain amount of jaw stretching and waggling, Lord Crouch spat it out.

'Very forceful woman, my sister!' he croaked, by way no doubt of apology. 'When she's roused.'

Forceful was not the word which sprang to Dover's mind but then, his vocabulary was naturally a good deal cruder than Lord Crouch's.

A writing pad was slapped on the table and a pencil all but poked out Dover's left eye. Lady Priscilla had returned.

'Oh, all right!' grumbled Dover, gazing at the writing instruments as though he feared they might up and bite him. He sighed. 'Well, what time did What's-his-name arrive on whenever it was?'

'About a quarter to six,' said Lady Priscilla before the muscles of Lord Crouch's mouth had even received the signal. 'And he left at approximately twenty past.'

Dover blew unpleasantly down his nose and scratched aimlessly on his writing pad. 'What happened after that?'

Lady Priscilla nobly yielded the floor to her brother. Lord Crouch thought long and deep. 'Gary and I had our – er – interview in the Malplaquet Library, don't you know. After he left, I went on working there. Accounts. Letters about bookings for coach parties. Hay for the zebras. That sort of thing.'

Dover passed a plump hand over a weary brow. 'Until when?'

Lord Crouch wove his legs elaborately round the legs of his chair. 'Oh, until about seven, I should think. Then I came up here. That's about right, isn't it, Prissy?'

'You were just in time for supper, Boys,' agreed Lady Priscilla, 'so it would be a minute or so before seven when you came up.'

'No alibi!' grunted Dover. It was a hollow triumph. He wrote the two words down in large black capitals. After a moment's hesitation, he drew a thick line underneath them.

Lord Crouch and Lady Priscilla watched the point of Dover's pencil as though hypnotized by it.

'Right!' said Dover, almost cheerfully. 'Well, that's that! Time for beddy-byes!' He kicked the brown shoes even further under the table and began to lever himself out of his chair.

'Don't you want Boys to sign his statement?' There seemed to be no end to Lady Priscilla's knowledge of police procedure.

Dover looked down at the writing pad and was inspired to make one of his better wriggles. 'Got to be typed out first,' he said.

Lady Priscilla still wasn't satisfied. 'Aren't you going to ask Boys what he and Gary talked about?' she asked, a faint frown creasing her well scrubbed forehead. 'After all, it might be significant, mightn't it?'

'For God's sake, Prissy!' exploded Lord Crouch, startling everybody as the words burst out with practically no hesitation. 'Why can't you mind your own damned business? And,' he added furiously as his vocal chords began seizing up again, 'keep your blasted mouth shut?'

It was the sort of thing that most detectives go down on their knees at night and pray for – the spontaneous, careless outburst. Any investigator worth his salt would have been after it like a terrier after a rabbit. Why didn't Lord Crouch wish to reveal the contents of his interview with the deceased? What guilty secret was he trying to hide? Was this the key destined to unlock the baffling mystery surrounding the death of Gary Marsh in Bluebell Wood?

Dover all but dislocated his jaw with an almighty yawn and wearily prepared to shoulder the burden that Lady Priscilla was forever foisting upon him. 'All right,' he said not even pretending that he gave a tinker's curse one way or the other, 'what did you talk about?'

The question was actually addressed to the ceiling but it was Lord Crouch who, after a few preliminary twitches and gulps, vouchsafed a reply. 'Oh, nothing of any very great importance.'

For some reason, Dover recalled a line he had heard in countless television plays. Apart from its aptness in the present situation, its very familiarity might serve to reassure Lady Priscilla. 'You had better,' recited Dover solemnly, 'let me be the judge of that, sir!' He immediately regretted the 'sir' but the courtesy slipped out before he could stop it.

A horrible gurgle bubbled up in Lord Crouch's throat.

Oh, 'strewth, thought Dover crossly, this was going to take all blooming night. But, as frequently happened when the chief inspector was in danger of being driven beyond all endurance, inspiration came most unfairly to his aid. It was something those damn-fool Tiffins or somebody had said. 'Didn't you talk about this motel thing you're supposed to be opening?'

Lord Crouch grabbed with pathetic eagerness for the life-line. 'Er – yes, that's it! The – er – motel. Yes, we discussed the motel.'

It was an answer that might not have satisfied a backward child of two, but it delighted Dover. He could now retire to his well-earned rest with a clear conscience and this time it was going to take more than Lady Priscilla's lah-di-dah blethering to stop him.

He got up from the table, a billow of grubby shirt escaping from the top of his trousers, and made a bee-line for the door. 'Right, well, that's settled that! Always a good idea to get these minor details cleared out of the way early on, eh?'

Lady Priscilla had recovered from her amazement and was on the point of shoving her aristocratic nose in again.

Dover struck first and struck hard. 'I'll have breakfast in bed in the morning,' he told her firmly. 'Nine o'clock sharp!' He got the door open before issuing his final instructions. 'And I don't want disturbing before then, not for nobody and not for nothing!'

Eleven

'The strain on the brain must be simply terrifying,' said Lady Priscilla in an awed whisper. 'And he had a most disturbed night. I doubt if the poor man got more than a wink of sleep.'

MacGregor, sitting uncomfortably at the kitchen table, regarded Lady Priscilla with genuine sympathy as she hovered by the cooker. She had, in fact, been hovering there for the best part of two hours, so anxious was she that Dover's breakfast should be ready when the fatal hour of nine o'clock struck. In spite of her earlier anxieties about over-sleeping, she had had no worries on that score. Thanks to Dover's innumerable visits to the bathroom during the previous night, nobody had been able to snatch much in the way of sleep and at six o'clock, as the overworked cistern had roared into life for the umpteenth time, Lady Priscilla had cut her losses and got up.

'I hope he didn't keep you awake,' said MacGregor politely.

Lady Priscilla smiled a wan smile, indicating that any martyrdom which had been inflicted on her was accepted with a contrite heart. During the long and noisy watches of the night Lady Priscilla had had ample time to review her attitude to Dover and gradually she had come to feel thoroughly ashamed of the antagonism she had shown him at her own dinner table. After all, who was she – a mere aristocrat – to criticize any member of the proletariat? Whatever other shortcomings she may have had, Lady Priscilla knew her place. And, in this modern, egalitarian society, it was right at the bottom of the pecking order. Not that Lady Priscilla was complaining. Far from it. Why, when you took everything into account, she and Boys were jolly lucky not to be swinging from the nearest lamp-post!

The more she thought about it, the more appalled Lady Priscilla had become. How could she have spoken to Chief Inspector Dover like that? How had she even dared to think that she could teach him his job? Fool that she was, she had been guilty of judging solely by appearances. She had seen the boorish, loutish exterior and totally missed the heart of gold that was beating underneath. She had noted the unhealthy complexion and the neanderthal brow – but what about the keen intelligence buzzing away behind? There are none so blind, Lady Priscilla told herself severely, as those who *won't* see!

'Were you late going to bed last night?' asked MacGregor, putting his watch to his ear to make sure it was still going.

'Not particularly.' Lady Priscilla stood back to admire the single plastic rose which she had found to adorn Dover's breakfast tray and gave it a finishing poke. 'Of course, it's the intensity of the effort that counts, not the hours, isn't it? What time is it now, sergeant?'

'Five to.'

'I think you'd better be making a move then.'

'Me?'

'The teapot is rather full so be careful not to spill it.'

'But, aren't you taking it in to him?' MacGregor tried, without being too rude about it, to push the tray back into Lady Priscilla's hands.

Lady Priscilla shook her head in gentle reproof. 'You forget I am not a married woman, sergeant! It would hardly be proper for me to invade a man's bedroom at this hour in the morning, would it?'

A short time later, as MacGregor stared fixedly at the view out of Dover's bedroom window, he could at least congratulate himself that he had spared Lady Priscilla this. From the bed behind him came the most life-like imitation of feeding time in the pig sty.

'That's the second night in a row I've been on the trot!' grumbled Dover through a mouth stuffed with food. 'It must be the air in this bloody place. And they've stuck the bog as far away as they possibly could.'

MacGregor spoke without turning his head. 'What are the plans for today, sir? I was wondering if we shouldn't . . .'

'I reckon it was that wine muck they gave me.' Dover tried, without much success, to salvage a blob of soft-boiled, free-range egg from the eiderdown. 'Like prussic acid swilling round in your gut. If you ask me, somebody ought to be prosecuted for it.'

'I really do think you should at least visit the scene of the crime, sir.'

'I don't know whether I shouldn't have the doctor,' said Dover glumly. 'There's such a thing as being too long suffering. And you get no thanks for it.'

Nobody could say that MacGregor gave up easily. 'And I've made a list of one or two people in the village, sir, who were on fairly friendly terms with Marsh. They may be able to . . .'

'Here!' yelped Dover. 'Take the tray!'

MacGregor swung round hopefully. 'Are you getting up, sir?'

'Not half!' said Dover, already out of bed. 'Gimme my overcoat!' His voice rose in panic. 'Quick, laddie!'

MacGregor had worked with Dover long enough to recognize an emergency when he saw one. Without a thought for personal hygiene he snatched up Dover's over-coat with his bare hands and thoughtlessly shouted, 'Come in!' in answer to an inopportune tap on the door.

Lady Priscilla duly came in and got an eyeful of Dover's elephantine hulk swathed only in his blue-striped, army surplus pyjamas. There were gasps of horror all round and Dover belatedly tried to preserve the decencies by grabbing his overcoat and holding it in front of him like a matador's cape.

'Good heavens!' breathed Lady Priscilla weakly.

Dover's reaction was more positive. 'Why the hell can't you knock, woman?'

MacGregor stepped neatly between them, just in case. 'Did you want something, Lady Priscilla?'

'Want something?' Lady Priscilla managed to avert her eyes from a sight which would have reconciled most un-married ladies to their solitary state and blinked bemusedly at MacGregor. 'Oh, yes, the telephone! Somebody wants to speak to the chief inspector. They wouldn't give a name.'

Dover had no time to spare for anonymous and – if past experience was anything to go by – probably abusive tele-phone calls. He had already delayed too long. Leaving MacGregor to cope with things, he set off with some urgency along the well-trodden path to the bathroom.

It was a quarter of an hour before he emerged. MacGregor was still standing patiently in the hall, holding the telephone.

MacGregor waited until the plumbing's death throes gurgled into an anguished silence. 'The caller insists that he will only speak to you, sir. He's still hanging on.'

Dover gloomily accepted the proffered receiver and handed his sergeant a short length of chain with a rubber ball on the end. 'Fix this back on for us!' he said. 'It just came off in my hand.'

MacGregor could find nothing to say and stalked off to the bathroom in a dignified silence. Dover pulled his overcoat tighter across the rolling acres of his paunch and addressed himself to his unknown caller.

'Wadderyewant?'

A man's voice replied. 'Is that Detective Chief Inspector Dover?'

No policeman worth his salt ever answers a question except by another question. Even policemen not worth their salt tend to adopt this infuriating habit.

'Who wants to know?'

'Never you mind!'

An impasse in bloody-mindedness appeared to have been reached and both contestants, breathing heavily, waited for the other to crack first. Dover won.

'You're the jack in charge of the Gary Marsh murder, aren't you?'

'Why do you ask?'

There was a sharp intake of breath at the other end of the line. 'I might have some information for you.'

'What did you say?' Dover temporarily shifted the receiver a few inches away from his head and explored the wax in his ear with the tip of his little finger.

The unseen caller counted silently up to ten. 'I said, I might have some information for you!'

Dover frowned. 'What about?'

'About the murder of Gary Marsh, for God's sake!'

'Oh.' Dover's frown deepened. 'Well, what is it?'

'Ah,' – the disembodied voice sounded fractionally happier, as though its owner thought they were getting somewhere at last – 'now, that's what we have to discuss, isn't it?'

'Is it?' Dover was already looking around for MacGregor. Well, 'strewth, he'd got better things to do with his time than stand around catching his death exchanging bon mots with gibbering lunatics.

The voice became gently chiding. 'Come on, Mr Dover, you know better than that!'

'Do I?' Dover sounded genuinely puzzled.

'I'll need a quid pro quo, won't I?' asked the voice insinuatingly.

Dover propped himself up against the wall, lost.

'Are you still there, Mr Dover?'

Dover grunted, unwilling to commit himself to a definite answer at this stage in the game.

'Now, listen, if I give you valuable information about Marsh's death, I'll want paying for it, won't I?'

Dover's as yet unshaven jaw dropped. This cheeky bugger was actually asking him for money! A quid, no less! Some people believed in setting their sights good and high.

The voice went thoughtlessly on. 'You get nothing for nothing in this world, Mr Dover.'

Dover was so affected by the simple truth of this assertion that he let slip a non-question. 'You can say that again, mate!'

'I'm glad you see it my way,' said the voice smoothly. 'I reckon you and me'll be able to come to some mutually acceptable arrangement. Shall we say half-past six tonight at The White Feathers? Saloon bar, of course.'

'Oh!' Dover suddenly began to see things in a different light. 'The White Feathers? Where's that?'

'In Claverhouse. Top of the High Street. You can't miss it.'

Dover had never missed a pub or a free booze-up in his life. His rosebud mouth contorted into a smile. 'Half-past six, you said?'

'Come alone!' instructed the unknown benefactor.

'Of course!' chuckled Dover, whose middle name was not generosity. 'Just a sec – how will I know you?' He didn't fancy the prospect of accosting a series of strangers in a public house. It was so easy to have one's motives misconstrued.

'Not to worry,' came the voice reassuringly, 'I shall know you!'

Dover listened to the dialling tone for quite a long time

before replacing the receiver. Oh, well, the day was turning out better than he would have ever dared to hope.

'Anything of importance, sir?' MacGregor had managed to replace the chain in the bathroom so that at least it looked all right.

'Just a chap with some information for me,' said Dover cagily, leading the way back to the bedroom. 'A tout.'

'Er – a *snout*, actually, sir.'

'That's what I said!' snapped Dover who didn't go much on having his jargon corrected by an underling. 'I've got to meet him tonight. Alone. But you'll have to drive me there.'

'Well, that sounds fine, sir. Just fine.' MacGregor was careful to hide his astonishment. It is an oft quoted axiom in police circles that a detective is only as good as his informants, which may help to explain the doldrums in which Dover's career had wallowed for so long. To the best of MacGregor's knowledge, Dover had never so much as seen an informer before, much less been contacted by one. Obviously the age of miracles was not yet over. 'Let's hope he'll be of some use to us, sir!'

Dover grunted and dropped his overcoat on the floor.

MacGregor stared at him in dismay. 'You're not going back to bed, sir?'

The springs squeaked and sagged. 'Blimey, I don't have to meet him till half-past six!'

'But ...'

Dover dragged the bedclothes up under his chin. 'This afternoon, laddie,' he promised sleepily. 'We'll take a little trip out somewhere this afternoon ... if it isn't raining.' He screwed his head deeper into the pillows. 'Don't slam the door!'

By the time, however, that MacGregor came back with his lunch, Dover had reached the sad conclusion that further sojourn in Lady Priscilla's spare bed would undoubtedly lead to permanent damage. The weather was still too inclement for any expedition in the open air to be feasible so Dover fell to wondering if there wasn't someone into whose life he could bring a little misery without exerting himself too much. There was always MacGregor, of course, but he could give MacGregor hell any old day of the week. No, what Dover fancied was a new victim, a fresh . . .

'Here!' He snapped his fingers with a panache that would have looked better coming from one of Lord Crouch's more cavalier ancestors. 'The landlord of that stinking little flea-pit of yours!'

'Mr Buckley, sir?' MacGregor put the locust-cleared luncheon tray down on the window seat.

'I want to see him. Right away. And sling my drawers over!'

MacGregor got hold of Dover's darned and yellowing long johns between a shrinking finger and thumb. 'The landlord of The Bull Reborn, sir?'

Dover was struggling out of his pyjama jacket to reveal an even yellower and more heavily darned vest. 'He knows more than he's saying.'

'Does he, sir?'

Dover dropped his pyjama trousers and MacGregor, whose mother had never wanted him to join the police, closed his eyes. 'Told you so, didn't I?' puffed Dover for whom getting dressed was a strenuous business. 'You've got a memory like a bloody sieve, you have!'

MacGregor didn't stand around arguing. Better to face an irate publican in the middle of his afternoon rest than remain a shuddering spectator at Dover's levé.

When, however, the landlord of The Bull Reborn was eventually ushered into Dover's presence, he was far more apprehensive than angry. He had already convinced himself that Dover was one hell of a tricky customer and the way the chief inspector was mouthing and gawping at him now did nothing to make him revise his opinion. The landlord was not to know that Dover couldn't remember for the life of him what he was supposed to be bullying this scurvy wretch about.

The landlord was not asked to sit down.

'All right!' snarled Dover in desperation. 'Spit it out!' Reclining like an obscene caricature of Madame Recamier on an old chaise longue, he raised one meaty fist to scratch his head.

The landlord cringed back. Well, the things you read in the newspapers!

Dover grinned devilishly. 'And get a move on!' he advised.

The landlord grovelled. 'It was just a friendly argument.'

'Not the story I heard,' lied Dover blandly. 'Still, we might as well hear your version.'

The landlord licked his parched lips and watched hopelessly as MacGregor got his notebook out. 'Well,' he began, 'it was Sunday lunch-time. The day Marsh was killed. In the bar. Marsh came in with Arthur Tiffin. They'd been to church. They started talking about Marsh's future prospects. He was going to marry Charmian Tiffin, you know.'

'I know everything,' said Dover modestly. 'So don't you try being funny with me or I'll have your guts for gaiters!'

The landlord paled and resumed his sorry tale. 'Well, I was serving behind the bar and we were pretty quiet so I couldn't help overhearing what they were sort of saying. After a bit, I heard 'em mention this blasted motel business. Well, I just saw red.'

'Why?' asked MacGregor as Dover seemed to be fully occupied with picking his nose.

The landlord was only too happy to air his grievances in a time and place that wouldn't give his bar trade the kiss of death. 'Oh, that bloody motel! What's it going to do to my business at The Bull, that's what I want to know? I don't care what stunts his lordship lays on here at Beltour, it's not going to generate enough trade for two catering establishments. I mean,' – he laughed uncertainly – 'it takes a murder to fill all our rooms up out of season now!'

This attempted touch of light relief didn't go down particularly well.

The landlord wiped his brow. 'Well, I couldn't forbear expressing my views to Mr Marsh. "You'll put me out of business," I told him. "You're cutting my throat!" He tried to pass it off. Said it was early days yet and Lord Crouch hadn't even got planning permission and they 'praps couldn't get a drinks licence anyhow. "Lord Crouch not get a drinks licence from our local bench?" I asked. "That'll be the day, by God it will!" Well, you can see my point of view, can't you? I wouldn't mind so much if Lord Crouch didn't pride himself on looking after us old soldiers. I mean, what's Gary Marsh ever done for his Queen and Country? I did my two years without a word of complaint – and in his lordship's own regiment. I'm an old South Shires Fusilier and you'd think that'd count for something, wouldn't you?'

'What happened next?' asked MacGregor.

'Eh? Oh, well – to cut a long story short – Marsh and me had a few more words about it and we both got a bit hot under the collar. Arthur Tiffin tried to calm us down and in the end Marsh sort of washed his hands of the whole affair. Said it hadn't anything to do with him. Well, that set me off again. I mean, I wasn't going to stand for that. "Nothing to do with you?" I said. "Everybody knows you're the one who's at the back of it. His lordship would never have thought of the idea if you hadn't suggested it to him first. Don't you tell me it's nothing to do with you, you sneaking little rat!" '

Dover could take just so much of this sort of thing, and no more. 'Get to the bloody point, can't you?'

The landlord looked hurt. 'But that is the point! Me and Marsh just had a friendly bit of an up-and-a-downer over this motel project.'

An expression of acute disgust oozed across Dover's face. 'And that's all?'

The landlord was stung to justify himself. 'I did threaten to break young Marsh's bloody neck for him,' he stoutly.

'Big deal!' Dover was plainly preparing to wash his hands of the whole business. 'Unfortunately, I don't happen to go around arresting people merely for shooting their stupid mouths off.'

Such sweet reasonableness not only took the wind out of the landlord's sails, but it floored Dover's long suffering assistant as well. MacGregor could recall numerous embarrassing occasions when his chief inspector hadn't had anything as substantial as idle threats to go on.

'I've no alibi,' the landlord pointed out helpfully. 'We don't open till seven on Sundays so I'd have had ample time to get back from Bluebell Wood, get myself cleaned down and open up.'

'Get yourself cleaned down?' MacGregor was clutching at straws but he had to try and make some progress somewhere. 'How did you know that the murderer was likely to be covered in mud?'

'Oh, come off it, sergeant!' the landlord chaffed in a rather patronizing way. 'Anybody round here knows it's ankle deep in mud round the Donkey Bridge at the best of times, never mind when we've had all this rain. Your murderer, whoever he is, would have been caked in muck up to his armpits, no matter how careful he was.'

MacGregor concentrated on not looking as though the only feeble shot in his locker had not just misfired. 'What happened after you threatened to break Marsh's neck for him?'

The landlord was getting almost as bored as Dover. He shrugged his shoulders. 'Nothing happened. It all calmed down. Another customer came in and I had to go and serve him. Arthur Tiffin took Marsh off to one of the tables and they finished their drinks there.'

'You didn't speak to Marsh again?'

'No. I'd said my piece. And, anyhow, I'll believe this motel scheme when I see it. Marsh had had enough, too. Every time I had to go near him and Tiffin, they kept their heads stuck close together and pretended they hadn't seen me. Even when I was as close to 'em as I am to you, they never so much as glanced at me.'

'Did you hear what they were talking about?' asked MacGregor, industriously spinning out the interview to a respectable length.

The landlord began to button up his coat. 'Oh, something about Henniford and Tuppeny Hill Camp. I only remember because those were my old stamping grounds. Tuppeny Hill Camp was the regimental depot of the South Shires and Henniford was where we lads used to go for a bit of night life. I suppose Arthur Tiffin was telling Marsh about the good old days when he was cutting a dash in a smart khaki uniform with a feather in his cap.'

MacGregor was reluctant to let the landlord go but in the end he had to. Dover's feelings were only too predictable.

'Jesus!' he sneered. 'You don't half give 'em a grilling when you're roused! Talk about putting 'em through it! For one minute there I thought you were going to clout him one with your handbag!'

MacGregor bit his lip. It was the rank unfairness of it all that choked him. You sat there, waiting until Dover had got himself into such a muddle that the old fool didn't know which day of the week it was and then, when you stepped in and tried to bring a bit of order into the proceedings, you got highly unoriginal abuse for your pains. MacGregor fell to wondering, as he frequently did, whether another appeal for clemency would do any good. Even the Assistant Commissioner (Crime) must have withers that could be wrung. It wasn't as though MacGregor was contemplating asking for anything out of this world – like promotion. He knew only too well that his long association with Dover the

Dead-Beat had put paid to any ambitions in that direction. Useless by association! No – all MacGregor wanted was a change. Anything would do, just as long as it was as far away as possible from the unspeakable old slob. 'One has to keep trying, sir,' he said huffily.

'Not when we get down to second-hand accounts of old soldier's beery reminiscences, we don't!' retorted Dover. 'If there's one thing I can live without, laddie, it's Arthur Tiffin's army memoirs!'

Twelve

MacGregor got Dover to The White Feathers at twenty-five past six on the dot. They sat side by side in the car park and stared out into the darkness. It was drizzling again and Dover seemed strangely on edge.

'I'll wait here for you, shall I, sir?'

Dover gnawed his bottom lip. 'Suppose so.'

'I'll come in with you, if you want, sir.'

'I can do without you sticking your nose in and buggering everything up!' The reply was a gem typical of Dover's conversational style but the chief inspector's heart wasn't really in it. He glanced round the car park nervously. 'You don't think it's a trap, do you?'

'A trap, sir?'

Dover fancied he detected a note of over-healthy scepticism in his sergeant's voice. 'Well, it bloody well could be!' he retorted hotly. 'Somebody murdered Marsh and it's common knowledge that I'm investigating the case. It wouldn't,' he added, breaking out in a cold sweat at the thought, 'be the first time a killer's tried to nobble me.'

MacGregor was reassuring. He felt he could well afford to be. 'Not in a saloon bar, sir. They'd have tried to lure you to some remote spot if they were intending to get rid of you.'

'Hm.' Dover still sounded unhappy. He sighed. 'Well, you just hang on here and keep your eyes skinned.' Reluctantly he opened the car door. 'And, if I'm not out in half an hour, come and get me!'

MacGregor watched Dover's seventeen and a quarter stones waddle slowly and painfully across the car park. Stupid old devil! As if any murderer in his right mind would try to rub him out! Dover was the best guarantee the criminal fraternity could possibly have that they would get away with it.

But MacGregor, in spite of having read no less than two books on popular psychology, had got it wrong. Dover was worried all right, but he wasn't really worried about his personal safety. Wild horses wouldn't have got him within a hundred miles of The White Feathers if he had been. No, the fear of assassination was merely a rationalization of a deeper and more fundamental terror. The truth was that Dover was constitutionally allergic to entering a public house all on his own. Usually he took every precaution to have somebody with him, somebody who could handle the delicate business of actually stepping up to the bar and ordering the drinks. But, now ... for one craven moment Dover almost packed it in and scuttled back to the sanctuary of the car. Horrible visions rose before his eyes. Suppose this fellow he was engaged to meet was late? Or didn't come at all? Would Dover be expected to purchase alcoholic beverages for a whole half hour while he waited?

The entrance to the saloon bar loomed up before him and Dover had to steel every nerve in his body before he could bring himself to push open the door. His heart plummeted as he stepped over the threshold. His worst fears had been realized for the bar was empty except for a couple of rather flashy women, desultorily dripping cigarette ash into their vodkas and lime. They automatically gave

Dover the once-over as he stood dithering in the doorway but they were hardened women of the world and knew a cheap skate when they saw one. They returned to discussing the various shortcomings of their husbands.

Dover closed the door behind him, taking as much time over it as he dared. A barmaid popped her head round the partition, saw that she had a new customer and came down the counter. She was quite a pleasant looking, motherly type of woman but she couldn't have produced a more paralyzing effect on Dover if she'd been old Medusa herself.

He answered her raised eyebrows and half smile with an ingratiating leer.

The barmaid tried again. 'Can I get you something, love?'

Dover shook his head with such violence that his jowls swung from side to side like pendulums gone beserk. 'Not at the moment,' he croaked. 'I'm – er – waiting for a friend.'

The barmaid had seen them come in all shapes and sizes and if this fat old scrounger thought he was going to make a convenience of her bar, he'd got another think coming. She was just about to explain the economics of the licensed victualler's trade when the door opened again and she decided to hold her peace, for the moment.

Dover turned eagerly in the pious hope that his salvation had arrived just in the nick. Apparently it had. A very small, wiry man, no longer in the first flush of youth, came whippily into the bar.

'Evening, Mr Dover!' he cried, extending his hand of friendship as though he had not only known Dover all his life but liked him, too.

Dover was equally effusive, with relief. 'Ah, good evening!'

'Nasty night!' commented the little man, rubbing his hands together.

'Stinking!' agreed Dover, removing his bowler hat and flinging back his overcoat. The saloon bar had suddenly become a warm and hospitable place.

The barmaid looked expectantly from one gentleman to the other. Both gentlemen studiously avoided catching her eye.

'Don't know what's happened to the weather these days,' said the little man, fixing his attention on a glass jar containing packets of potato crisps. 'It never used to be like this.'

Dover was busy reading the advertisement displayed round the rim of an ashtray. 'It certainly didn't,' he agreed.

The barmaid got fed up. 'Can I get you something?' she asked.

The little man turned hopefully to Dover only to find that Dover was turning equally hopefully towards him. It was a situation that called for action.

The little man nodded reassuringly at the barmaid. 'Just a sec, ducks,' he said and beckoned Dover down to the far end of the counter where the problem could be resolved in comparative privacy.

Dover inclined an apprehensive ear.

'You,' hissed the little man, 'are supposed to buy the drinks!'

'Me?' Dover goggled, dismayed at such bluntness.

'Of course! It's always the scuffers what pay.'

'Is it?' Dover felt sick. 'Are you sure?'

The little man bounced up and down with frustration. 'Sure I'm sure! Look, don't start coming the old soldier with me, squire! You know the score!'

Dover nodded – though what the effort cost him no-one will ever know – and the pair of them trooped back down the bar to where the barmaid was still waiting.

Dover coughed a harsh, dry cough but the unaccustomed words still stuck in his throat.

'Well?' demanded the barmaid who was beginning to doubt the evidence of both her eyes and her ears.

Dover swallowed hard and turned to his companion. 'What,' he rasped in a strangled voice, 'is yours?'

Men have been awarded the Victoria Cross for less.

'I'll have a double scotch!' said the little man quickly.

Dover clutched the counter. When his head had cleared he found that the blasted woman was still waiting.

'And the same for you, sir?'

Dover's morale had taken a severe pounding but he could imagine how much two large whiskies would cost. A bloody king's ransom! 'I'll have a small bottle of ginger ale!' he gasped.

The barmaid wasn't going to argue. She got the drinks and accepted a pound note from Dover's trembling hand as though it was the most natural thing in the world.

'We'll go and sit down over there,' said the little man, taking Dover firmly by the arm and preventing him from counting his change for the third time.

Dover allowed himself to be steered into a corner alcove. He still couldn't believe that two lousy drinks had . . .

'Cheers!' said the little man who, in spite of a certain savoir faire, clearly had his blind spots.

Dover pulled himself together and took a solemn vow to get even. 'What's your name?' he demanded.

The little man's eyes twinkled. 'Call me Josh, squire!'

Glumly Dover watched the bubbles rise in his ginger ale. 'Well, what have you got to tell me?'

'Ah, now that depends on whether you're prepared to make it worth my while, don't it? I mean, I'm taking a risk, coming here and talking to you like this.'

Dover had few scruples at the best of times but, where Josh was concerned, he had none. 'How much?'

The little man pursed his lips and tried to calculate what the market would stand. 'Twenty nicker?' he asked doubtfully.

'You're on!' said Dover.

The little man relaxed and removed his muffler to reveal a very crumpled bow tie and a small battered metal badge in the lapel of his jacket. He was relieved that the tiresome preliminaries were now over. So relieved, in fact, and so eager to rat, that he failed to ask for any more surety for his twenty pounds than Dover's unsupported word. 'Ah,' – he beamed happily – 'it's a pleasure to do business with you, squire! You're a man after my own heart, straight you are!'

Dover grimly kept his mouth shut and let the insult go unchallenged.

Little Josh took another sip at his whisky and smacked his lips appreciatively, a sound which pierced Dover to the heart. 'Well, now,' he began cheerfully, 'I daresay you've been spending a fair bit of time these last couple of days trying to find out what sort of a joker Gary Marsh really was, eh? Asking his auntie and his girl friend and Lord Crouch and Uncle Tom Cobley and all, eh? Well, whatever yarns they spun you, forget 'em!'

Dover raised his eyebrows.

Josh chuckled. 'Would you believe wine, women and song?'

Dover thought it over. 'No.'

Josh's chuckles became estatic. 'I knew it! Soon as I laid eyes on you, I knew you weren't as thick as you look, squire!'

Dover received the compliment with little pleasure. 'Get on with it!' he warned.

'Marsh was short of the ready,' muttered Josh sulkily.

'Who isn't?'

'Ah, but he didn't just sit back and moan about it. He was a bright lad. He went out and did something about it.'

Dover frowned. 'You a friend of Marsh?' he asked.

'Hell, no!' Josh could see the gaping chasm opening in front of that question. 'Don't you try and pin anything on me, squire! I've only spoken a couple of words with him in my life.'

'Then how come you know so much about him?'

'Ah, well, that's my job, isn't it?'

'Is it?' said Dover.

Josh grinned again and leaned forward so that his words

should fall exclusively into Dover's ears. 'I'm what you might call the trouble-shooter for Taffy O'Sullivan,' he whispered proudly.

'Taffy O'Sullivan?'

'The bookie! Oh, come off it, squire! You'll be telling me next you've never heard of him. Taffy O'Sullivan! The bookie! He's the coming man in the betting shop world, believe you me. Three branches scattered throughout the country already. Give that boy another couple of years and he'll have the betting scene tied up so tight they won't know what's hit 'em.'

Dover sat down heavily on Josh's euphoria. 'He's news to me. Here, are you telling me that Marsh was a betting man?'

'He'd have had a wager on two bloody raindrops trickling down a windowpane.'

Dover absentmindedly abstracted a cigarette from the packet Josh had thoughtlessly deposited on the table while he searched for his matches. 'First I've heard about it,' he grumbled.

'Well, of course it is, squire!' said Josh eagerly as he gave Dover a light. 'I told you, they don't know nothing in Beltour. Mind you, Marsh did his level best to keep it all a dark secret. That auntie of his would have killed him if she'd known the half of what sonnie-boy was up to. Bloody unfair, really, because when you come to think about it, it was her what drove him to it.'

Dover thoughtfully blew a mouthful of smoke into Josh's face. 'How d'you mean?'

Josh rubbed his finger and thumb together in an expressive mime. 'Money, squire! She'd got Marsh by the short hairs. He had to hand his wage packet over to her every week and she collared the bleeding lot, apart from a couple of quid or so she gave him back for pocket money. Well, what can you do with a couple of lousy quid, these days?'

'Not much!' said Dover, remembering with feeling what one round of drinks had cost him.

'So, six days a week, you might say, Marsh was dead skint. And there was nothing he could do about it. He couldn't hold out on auntie, see, because she was fly enough to check his pay-slip every time. Of course, what really got Marsh's goat was that he was actually worth a packet. Auntie used to stash away his money in the bank for him, see, but she'd fixed it somehow so's he couldn't get his hot little hands on it without her say-so.'

'So Marsh started betting to try and make some money?'

Josh nodded. 'Poor sucker! Mind you, it didn't work. Well, it never does, does it? The only jokers who make money out of the gee-gees are the bleeding bookies.'

'And that's where you came in?'

Josh nodded again. 'He was in to Taffy O'Sullivan for nearly forty quid. And that's a lot of money in anybody's book.'

Dover swirled the dregs of his ginger beer round in his glass. 'So you put the frighteners on him?'

'I did not!' Josh was highly indignant. 'Do I look like one of your strong arm mob, for God's sake? Besides, that's not Taffy O'Sullivan's style – well, not until everything else has failed, it isn't. No, I approached Marsh – a week before he cashed his chips in, it'd be – on a reasonable man-to-man basis and told him if he didn't cough up toot sweet I'd have to go to his auntie for the cash. Worked better than a kick in the guts, that did. Christ, you should have seen his face!'

'He paid up?'

Josh averted his eyes sheepishly. 'Well, no, not actually.'

'Not actually?' snorted Dover. 'What the hell's that supposed to mean?'

'He didn't pay up at all,' muttered Josh.

'So?'

Josh's tiny face hardened. 'So Taffy O'Sullivan didn't like it one bloody bit, did he? Blamed it all on me, the lousy bastard. Give me over the weekend to get the cash or he'd have me carved up when they did Marsh. I was at my bleeding wits' end, I can tell you. I'd asked a few questions round about Miss Marsh and I reckoned it was a waste of time trying to put the screws on her. She'd have set the cops on me, soon as look at me. I had another go at Marsh, of course, but you can't get blood out of a stone. All that welsher could suggest was that I waited till he got married because his auntie'd promised to let him look after his own bleeding money then. Jesus! I asked him if he couldn't touch his girl friend's family for a bob or two, but he didn't like the sound of that. Thought the Tiffins might cut up rough if they found out they were going to have a gambler for a son-in-law.' Josh sighed. 'Poor bugger! I could feel for him. I've been in the same fix myself a couple of times and I know what it's like. Soon as you ask 'em for a bit of a helping hand, they start looking at you like you're something that's crawled out from under a bloody stone.'

Dover consulted the bar clock again and turned back to Josh with some weariness. 'When did you speak to him?'

'To Marsh? The Friday night before he was croaked on the Sunday. I finally caught up with him at the bus station in Claverhouse here. Ruined my bleeding weekend, it did,' he added resentfully.

Dover scratched his head and then studied his fingernails with considerable interest.

'Still,' – Josh had a basically optimistic nature and never let things get him down for long – 'every cloud has a silver lining.'

Not in Dover's experience it didn't. He invited Josh to explain.

'Well, Marsh went and got himself bumped off, didn't he? Believe you me, squire, I started breathing again when I heard that bit of news.'

'Oh?'

'Well, it wiped the slate clean, didn't it?'

Dover eyed Josh with intense dislike. 'Did it?'

'Of course it did!' Little Josh seemed impressed in spite of himself. 'Rule of the house with Taffy O'Sullivan! All outstanding debts cancelled if a client dies on him. Well, up to a couple of hundred, anyhow. Taffy O'Sullivan runs a very classy business, you know.'

There is no doubt – well, not much – that Dover would have followed up this interesting development if he hadn't been fatally distracted by the way Josh was rattling his empty glass on the table top. It was a hint Dover himself had dropped too often not to know what it signified and he was infused with fury. If this little rat thought he was going to get another double whisky, he was about to be sadly disappointed. By the time Dover had got over his irritation at Josh's presumption, he'd forgotten what they were talking about.

Josh once again pushed his glass into what he hoped was Dover's line of vision. 'So you'll give O'Sullivan the works, will you?'

'Might,' said Dover, gloomily unhelpful.

'Might?' Josh was horrified. 'Look, I'm telling you, squire – it's that rat O'Sullivan you want. The lousy punk's been chucking his weight around for years. It's about time somebody put him through it for a change. Besides,' – he glanced round nervously – 'what's going to happen to me? He'll gut me! I'd have never come within a mile of you if I hadn't thought you were going to fix him. Look, you've got to run him in, squire, and bloody quick.'

Dover scowled. 'You trying to teach me my job?'

' 'Course not, squire!' Josh managed an ingratiating smile. 'I'm just trying to help you, aren't I? But you can't blame me for trying to save my own neck, can you? I'm telling you, you don't know what a murdering bastard Taffy O'Sullivan is. He'll stop at nothing and, if he thought for a moment I'd ...'

'Oh, shut up!' said Dover.

Thirteen

MacGregor came back from the bar and placed a foaming tankard of best bitter in front of his lord and master.

Dover clutched it with both paws. ' 'Strewth,' he exclaimed, 'I reckon I've earned this!'

MacGregor slid into the seat on the opposite side of the table and hid his face as best he could in a glass of dry sherry. Everybody in the bar was staring at them – and with good reason. For five glorious minutes there had been more excitement in the saloon bar than those smoke-stained walls had seen since the place opened.

The real fun and games had begun when a bewildered Josh finally realized that Dover wasn't going to pay over the promised twenty nicker. The little man took the disappointment badly. His voice grew louder and louder as the aspersions he began casting on Dover's honour and ancestry got nastier and nastier. Indeed, so angry did he become that Dover, in spite of the marked difference in their respective fighting weights, began to fear physical violence.

'You great fat double-crossing old welsher!' screamed Josh, leaping to his feet and banging his little fists on the table. 'You're cheating me, that's what you're bloody well doing! Well,' – he sucked in a steadying lungful of air – 'you won't get away with it! I'll get even with you, you swindling old bugger, if it's the last thing I do!'

'Oh, shove off!' urged Dover, shuffling awkwardly along his bench so as to keep the table between himself and Josh. 'I'll run you in for causing a disturbance, else,' he threatened.

Josh got his second wind. 'You'll run me in?' he repeated scornfully. 'You and whose regiment, mate!' He leaned forward across the table and thrust his tiny, flushed face to within an insulting couple of inches of Dover's nose. 'You lay so much as one finger on me, you over-blown baboon, and I'll . . .'

Posterity, and the handful of fascinated gawpers in the saloon bar, never discovered what dire threat Josh had in mind because it was at this precise moment that MacGregor came mincing diffidently to the rescue. He had been hovering outside the door for some time, waiting with an anxious eye on the second hand of his watch. When Dover said half an hour, he occasionally meant half an hour.

'Chuck him out!' shouted Dover, growing more resolute when he saw that MacGregor had got a firm grip on Josh's collar. 'Get shut of him!'

Josh twisted round and spat his next threat as best he could into MacGregor's face. 'I'll have you for bleeding assault, sonnie! You want to watch it, you do! I've got witnesses!'

The hitherto avid spectators had other ideas, though. They turned away immediately and became deeply engrossed in their own affairs. Well, a bit of excitement was a bit of excitement, but one didn't want to get involved, did one?

MacGregor, meanwhile, was busy propelling a dangling Josh towards the exit. 'You just keep quiet!' he advised sternly. 'And don't come round bothering Mr Dover again or it'll be the worse for you.'

Josh clutched at a partition in passing. 'Bother that old pig again?' he gasped. 'You must be joking!' His grasping fingers were inevitably dragged away and from then on things began to happen rather quickly. MacGregor, skilfully avoiding all Josh's attempts to put the boot in where it matters, got the saloon bar door open and the poor little man had barely time to bestow a few more pieces of his vulgar mind on Dover before he found himself sprawling on the cold, hard ground outside.

'Drunk as a lord,' said Dover as MacGregor came back, fastidiously brushing himself down. 'As if I was going to hand over twenty quid to a cheap little rat like him.'

MacGregor loudly said nothing, letting the disapproval on his face speak for him. Detectives may not like informers, but they are under a moral obligation to keep faith with them. Dover, as usual, had let the side down and had let it down – MacGregor became conscious of the watching eyes – in full view of the general public. Oh, it was so absolutely mortifying!

Dover was quick to notice that his sergeant was standing there doing nothing. 'I'll have a pint of bitter!' he said.

MacGregor marched off stiffly to get the drinks.

'Well, sir,' he said, when Dover's unsavoury face eventually emerged with a large white moustache obliterating his small black one, 'did you get any information out of him?'

Dover set his glass down, his good humour evaporating with the speed of light. He liked MacGregor's cheek, by God he did! Whatever scraps of miserable information had been obtained from that drink-sodden midget had been purchased – by Dover – at a high price. It was typical of MacGregor to come strolling along when it was all over and expect to reap the fruits of another man's work for free! The way he was going on you'd think bloody double whiskies grew on trees.

Dover sank resentfully beneath the froth again. 'Gurgle-sloshlurp!' he said.

'Sir?'

'I said, nothing much!' snapped Dover.

'Oh, well, I'm not surprised,' said MacGregor with that faintly knowing air that made Dover see red.

The chief inspector was stung to hasty retaliation. 'Did you know that Marsh was up to his ears in debt to a bookie?' he demanded.

'No, sir. But, surely,' – MacGregor smiled a superior little smile – 'surely you don't think that this is some sort of Chicago style, mobster killing, do you, sir?'

'It's as good a theory as any that you've come up with!' snarled Dover. 'In any case, you'd better get up off your backside and do some investigating.'

MacGregor's gentle scepticism was quite unruffled. 'Do you by any chance remember the bookie's name, sir?'

'Taffy O'Sullivan!' said Dover, astounding them both by the sharpness of his memory. He watched with contempt as MacGregor duly got his notebook out and then, losing interest, let his eyes wander round the bar. Over in one corner he noticed for the first time that there were a couple of brightly glowing fruit machines. Dover's face brightened to match. 'Got any change, laddie?'

'I think so, sir.' MacGregor snapped his notebook shut and wondered what old bird-brain was up to now.

Dover got to his feet and began to lumber across the room. 'You can get some more at the bar,' he said.

It eventually cost MacGregor the best part of three pounds to learn that Dover had managed to acquire no less than two new murder suspects. There was Taffy O'Sullivan and little Josh himself. That he should have achieved this in a mere half hour probably, thought MacGregor wiltingly, constituted a record.

Bored well nigh to tears, MacGregor watched his ten-penny pieces disappearing down the greedy slot of the one-armed bandit and listened while Dover, in between dragging the lever down and kicking the machine when it failed to disgorge, expounded his theories.

'That undersized little twerp,' Dover began.

'Josh, sir,' prompted MacGregor.

'So he said.' Dover paused while he waited for the spinning symbols to stop. A plum, a bell and a cherry slotted into the windows. He consulted the table of winning combinations. Just his bloody luck! 'Anyhow, he's got a motive for murder. Taffy O'Sullivan was threatening to duff him up if he didn't collect that money from Marsh, but Josh' – Dover broke off to feed another coin into the fruit machine – 'Josh knew that O'Sullivan cancelled all debts if one of his punters died on him.'

MacGregor witheld comment until Dover had recovered from the exertion of working the lever. 'So Josh was let off the hook? Well, I suppose it's a possibility, sir.' MacGregor prided himself on his tact. 'Er – did you think to ask Josh to account for his whereabouts at the time of the murder, by any chance?'

' 'Strewth,' grunted Dover, thumping the machine in the hope of inducing it to play the game, 'I can't be expected to do all the flaming work, laddie! You'll have to follow it up. Sometime.'

'Yes, sir,' said MacGregor, telling himself that chance would be a fine thing. 'And you think this Taffy O'Sullivan might be involved, too?'

'Could be.' Dover was re-reading the instructions. Damn it all, it looked simple enough! 'Marsh owed him money and wouldn't pay. No bookie worth his salt can afford to let people get away with that sort of thing. He sent Josh to collect and got damn all for his pains. Not surprising if he turns to something a bit rougher. They probably only meant to beat What's-his-name up but they went too far and he got killed by mistake.'

'Yes, sir.' MacGregor sometimes had bad dreams in which Dover solved his case by sticking a pin in the telephone directory and applying for a warrant. 'Well, I suppose that's a possibility, too.'

The want of enthusiasm did not go unmarked. 'Oh, don't rupture yourself!' growled Dover, exploiting a rich vein of heavy sarcasm.

'Well, sir, we do seem to be collecting rather a lot of suspects but very little evidence. I mean, you've already got your eye on Miss Marsh and Lord Crouch, the whole Tiffin family, the landlord of The Bull Reborn and – oh – and Lady Priscilla.' MacGregor was staring mesmerized at the spinning symbols. 'Now we've got this Josh character and Taffy O'Sullivan, the bookie. It does seem rather a lot, doesn't it, sir?'

'I've run out of change,' said Dover.

MacGregor pulled himself together, went back to the bar and handed over another pound note.

Dover accepted the handful of coins sullenly. 'I reckon this machine's crooked,' he said as he cast his next piece of bread on the ungrateful waters.

MacGregor sat himself on the edge of a table. They were obviously going to spend the rest of the evening stuck in The White Feathers so he might as well make himself comfortable. 'What's our next move, sir?'

Dover didn't have time to voice his resentment at this continual harassment because, miracle of miracles, a couple of coins unexpectedly tinkled down into the cup. 'Whacko!' he said and was just about to pocket his winnings when he noticed that they were not legal tender. 'Here,' he roared furiously, 'I've been done!'

Patiently MacGregor abandoned the murder of Gary Marsh and explained to Dover that the coins were tokens which could only be used for purchases across the bar.

'It's a bloody swindle!' objected Dover. 'Oh, well, you'd better buy 'em off me. They're no damned good to me. You can use 'em for the next round of drinks.'

Success, even to the modest tune of five new pence, didn't

strike again and Dover was not a good loser. By about half past eight the pleasures of chucking MacGregor's good money down the drain were beginning to pall. Dover tugged down the handle on positively his last attempt to win fame and fortune, examined the line of two plums and a lemon and directed his mind to higher things.

He turned to MacGregor. 'We'll go and have a bit to eat somewhere,' he announced. 'I'm bloody starving.'

'Very good, sir.'

'And then' – Dover flexed his shoulders. 'Strewth, it took it out of you, yanking that lever thing. – 'we might go and tackle old Crouch.'

MacGregor registered surprise and not a little apprehension. 'Sir?'

'Suppose,' said Dover, leaning on the one-armed bandit and trying to ease the weight on his feet, 'there was something between him and Marsh?'

MacGregor gave the suggestion more consideration than it merited. 'What sort of a something, sir?'

'Couple of pansies!' explained Dover with a snigger. 'The idea came to me just now, seeing you standing there like a drooping arum lily. It would explain everything, wouldn't it? Like old Crouch giving him that posh job.'

'Managing the motel, sir?'

'Marsh was the wettest thing since nappies,' said Dover. 'Even old Crouch'd never think of employing him if he wasn't besotted with the lad.'

'There is the theory that Marsh was Lord Crouch's illegitimate son – or nephew,' MacGregor pointed out unhappily. 'And then, again, for all we know, Marsh may have been extremely competent at his job.'

Dover, having buttoned up his overcoat, now appeared totally engrossed in trying to scrape off one of the more disgusting stains on the lapel. 'You don't reckon old Crouch is one of the nancy boys?' he asked slyly.

MacGregor achieved a thin smile. 'Hardly, sir.'

Dover took the demolition of his latest crack-pot theory with remarkable equanimity. 'Oh, well,' he said, 'I reckon I'll have to take your word for it, shan't I? After all, they do say it takes one to spot one, don't they?'

Fourteen

Luckily, by the time our hero got back to Beltour and had crawled on his hands and knees up to the Crouch's eyrie, all thoughts of tackling anything but bed had long since seeped out of his mind.

The following morning it dawned so gorgeous and spring-like that even Dover got round to feeling that it might be a shame to remain indoors. This enthusiasm for the open air life was reinforced by the departure, before he could be stopped, of Lord Crouch to some business meeting in London and by the determination of Lady Priscilla to make a start on her spring cleaning. Dover, the weeniest bit hung-over after his excesses of the night before, found the monotonous drone of the vacuum cleaner more than his head could stand and so, all in all, the rural delights of Donkey Bridge and Bluebell Wood proved irresistible.

MacGregor naturally didn't choose to point out to Dover that he had left it a little late in the day to start viewing the scene of the crime. Heaven only knows, there had not been much to see in the first place but, since then, everything had been determinedly trampled flat for yards and yards around. However, physical effort on Dover's part was such a rare plant that MacGregor considered himself under a moral obligation to foster it whenever he could. He drove Dover as near as possible and then encouragingly made light of the few hundred yards which would have to be covered on foot.

Dover rolled along the fatal path almost happily. The sun was warm, but not oppressively so, the trees were bursting into bud and a few birds were singing. 'You should have brought a picnic basket!' he told MacGregor, just so that young gentleman should remember that there is a rift in every lute.

They penetrated deeper into the wood. The going became harder. The path grew muddier and tree roots poked up awkwardly to catch at unwary feet. The occasional oath started to explode in the balmy air. MacGregor offered his arm and Dover grabbed it without gratitude, holding on like a nervous limpet until they reached the Donkey Bridge itself.

The bridge was an unpretentious, plank construction, erected for the sole purpose of crossing a small stream which sparkled and bubbled along a shallow, rock strewn bed.

'Very picturesque,' sniffed Dover, lowering his weight gratefully on to one of the uneven stone slabs which formed the steps up to the bridge. 'Where was the body?'

MacGregor indicated a confused and trampled depression by the side of the stream. 'Just there, sir!' Being MacGregor, of course, he couldn't leave it there. He had brought his brief case with him and now conscientiously produced a whole series of starkly factual police photographs for Dover's delight and edification.

Dover eyed the pictures of the rain-sodden, mud splashed and battered body queasily. Dead bodies – even photographs of dead bodies – always played hell with his sensitive stomach. MacGregor, however, was still waiting optimistically for some pearl of wisdom to fall from the master's lips. Dover did not disappoint him. 'Got a fag, laddie?' he asked.

MacGregor all but snatched his precious photographs

back and got his cigarettes out. 'Judging by the injuries, sir,' he went on doggedly in the face of Dover's massive indifference, 'the murderer must have been standing up there on the edge of the bridge when he struck the blows that killed Marsh.' Almost in spite of himself Dover half turned to gawp at the spot which MacGregor was indicating with a beautifully manicured index finger. It was a little above where the chief inspector was sitting. 'That's right, sir, about there. If you could just move a second, sir, I could show you exactly . . .'

'Don't bother!' growled Dover. 'I've got the bloody picture.' He looked round stupidly. 'What about the murder weapon?'

MacGregor managed a wintry little smile. Another minute and the old fool would be asking him who the victim was. 'I believe I did tell you about that earlier, sir, didn't I?'

Dover scowled one of his blackest scowls. 'Refresh my memory!' he invited.

'It was, we think, a piece of railing torn off the bridge. You can see that it's all rotten and broken. It would be easy enough to pull a sizeable chunk off.'

Dover sighed and let his podgy body sag despondently. The stone step upon which he was sitting was hard, and damp. Much more of this and he'd be adding piles to his already lengthy list of sociably unacceptable ailments. It was time to call it a day. He was just about to demand MacGregor's assistance in helping him to his feet when his attention was distracted by the clatter of tiny hooves approaching down the path. Another second and one of the zebras came skittering to a startled halt. Dover, no animal lover at the best of times, didn't even attempt to resist this heaven sent temptation. With a speed he would have thought well-nigh suicidal in any other circumstances, he snatched up a handy-sized stone. The zebra, no fool, tried to make a run for it but failed to get its striped bottom out of range in time. Bellowing indignantly, it shot back down the path from whence it had come.

Dover dusted off his hands. 'That'll learn it!' he sniggered, delighted at the look of dismay on MacGregor's face. 'Well, anything else, laddie?'

MacGregor, beyond words, shook his head and helped Dover to his feet. 'We're going back to the car now, are we, sir?'

But Dover was nothing if not perverse. He had fully intended returning to the car until MacGregor mentioned it. Now he had to think of something else. 'Which way did the murderer come?'

'Well, of course, that's what we really don't know, sir. You can see what the ground's like round here and with all that rain. . . . As I said before, sir, it is possible that Marsh was followed, or even accompanied, from Beltour House, but my theory is that the killer approached from the opposite direction.' Here Dover blew out his lips in what might have been a lethargic raspberry but MacGregor refused to rise to the implied comment on his powers of deduction. 'I feel that he must have got here ahead of Marsh and the obvious thing is that he came towards him from the direction of the railway station. That does imply a certain degree of premeditation, I suppose, but I can't see any objection to that. In any case, whether it was a murder of impulse or something that had been planned well in advance, it still remains as big a mystery as ever, doesn't it, sir?'

Dover fancied he detected a note of criticism in his sergeant's voice and jumped to quash it. 'It's no bloody mystery to me!' he snorted. 'Lord Crouch is our man.' Nobody could fault Dover when it came to pig-headedness.

'Well, not if my theory is correct, sir. I mean, according to all the evidence we have at the moment, the only way Lord Crouch and Marsh could have been here at the Donkey Bridge together on Sunday evening was if they'd walked here together from the house.'

Dover had twisted round and was staring across the bridge. 'Where does this path go, anyhow?' he asked.

MacGregor repressed the urge to let lightning strike twice in the same place by smashing Dover's stupid head in with a piece of railing but he wasn't yet quite prepared to serve a life sentence for the infuriating old fool. He unclenched his teeth sufficiently to say. 'To the railway station, sir!'

'Oh, yes.' Dover vaguely remembered somebody mentioning something about a railway station. Uninteresting sort of place. Still, beggars can't be choosers. 'Come on!' he said. 'We'll go and see.'

The Donkey Bridge buckled dangerously as Dover's weight trundled across it but the ancient timbers stood up to the strain. Across the bridge, the path rose gently and Dover, assisted by some timely shoving from his sergeant, puffed slowly up it. Halfway he paused for breath and reflection. 'Somebody,' he panted, 'must have hated What's-his-name's guts to tackle this lot. And in the dark. It's like a bloody assault course.'

They plodded on and, when the going became easier, Dover began to look around. The wood, always small and never really dense, was thinning out and the village of Beltour could be clearly seen through the straggling branches. It was surprisingly near. The church steeple and the roofs of the taller houses rose rather charmingly into the blue sky.

A little further along the path forked and Dover took the opportunity to stop and have another little rest. 'You didn't,' he pointed out accusingly, 'tell me there was two paths.'

MacGregor simply hadn't wanted to make things too complicated. He blushed, however, and hastened to rectify his omission. 'The right hand fork is the one that goes to the railway station, sir. This one on the left goes to the village.'

Dover sniffed. 'Proper little encyclopedia, aren't you?'

'I have explored both paths, sir,' explained MacGregor, still smarting. 'The murderer could have approached the

Donkey Bridge along either, of course. One imagines that he probably came from the village but, of course, there's no evidence either way.'

'That's the trouble with this bloody case,' said Dover, rejecting the pleasures of tearing a strip off MacGregor in favour of a good old grumble. 'No bloody clues. 'Strewth, you'd have thought there'd have been a footprint or a cigarette packet or something to give us a lead.'

MacGregor felt obliged to point out a basic fact which appeared to have escaped Dover's notice. 'We wouldn't have been called in, sir, if the identity of the murderer had been obvious.'

'Trust you to start finding excuses!' muttered Dover. 'Well, come on then! No point in standing around here all blooming morning.' And, so saying, he set off along the path which led to the village.

MacGregor strolled along behind.

The path was muddy here, too, and both Dover and MacGregor had their work cut out to keep their balance. Before they had gone more than a few yards, Dover slammed on the brakes again. 'We might,' he said, 'get a cup of coffee somewhere.'

The Bull Reborn, thanks to the ginger cat's vendetta, was presumably out of bounds. 'There is a rather grubby little snack bar, sir,' said MacGregor cautiously.

'It'll do!' responded Dover, who cared naught for hygiene, and proceeded on his way with renewed vigour in his step. Nothing was more calculated to raise his spirits than the imminent prospect of food and drink, especially after one of Lady Priscilla's meagre, nut-cutlet breakfasts. Dover fell to musing on whether or not it might be worth breaking with tradition and dropping his wife a postcard, demanding the immediate despatch of food parcels.

They reached the church, an undistinguished building for which an earlier Lord Crouch had footed the bill. Dover, out of breath again, leaned on the wall and contemplated the gravestones. Some buggers had all the luck! Having nothing better to do, he read the inscription on the nearest headstone and lingered enviously over the final words: Rest in Peace. It wasn't that Dover had a death wish or anything kinky like that. It was just that he was drawn irresistibly to the horizontal and the motionless.

The first drops of rain came spattering down. 'Oh, hell!' said Dover.

There were not many things which would induce the chief inspector to enter a church, but a heavy shower of rain happened to be one of them. MacGregor, trailing unwillingly along behind and possessing at least the rudiments of correct behaviour, managed to whip off Dover's bowler hat before the proprieties were offended. They sat down in a pew to wait until the heavens should close again.

It was dark inside the church and for a few moments the claps of thunder rolling around outside smothered all other sounds. It was only when this died away that MacGregor realized that they were not alone. Up by the altar a couple of embarrassed tourists were getting an unsolicited tour from the vicar. Currently they were paying rather less attention to the glories of a large stained glass window (c.1924 and sacred to the memory of Queenie Benckenbinder Crouch) than to the problem of whether and, if so, how much to tip the importunate cleric when he finally allowed them to make their escape. They needn't have worried. The vicar himself was not in the least squeamish about these delicate financial transactions. Quite a number of the visitors to Beltour House popped into the village church on the off chance that it might contain something worth looking at. It didn't, but even rubbish needs money for its upkeep and the earlier Lord Crouch had been a mite stingy with his endowments. Nor did the vicar reckon on giving his services for free. Having talked long enough and spent long enough with the tourists to put them into his debt, he left them with a smiling and precise description of where the various boxes were for the Poor, the Church Fabric, the Roof, the Flower Fund and the Foreign Missions.

'No obligation, of course!' he leered and, gathering up his skirts, swept majestically down the centre aisle to corral the new arrivals.

Dover lost no time in disillusioning him.

The vicar didn't mind at all. An ex-Army padre, he was very keen on uniforms and the maintenance of law and order and delighted to meet a couple of chaps who shared his attitude. In the gloom of the church Dover's unspeakable scruffiness and bolshie expression were not immediately discernible.

The vicar sat down companionably in the next pew. 'Well, we shall give the poor lad a good send-off at all events,' he said happily. 'The funeral's tomorrow, you know. Would you like me to reserve you a couple of seats? I'm expecting a full house so it's advisable to book!' He rubbed his hands together gleefully. 'I hear they're running a couple of coaches over from Claverhouse. With a bit of luck and if this weather clears, it could be standing room only.'

'I suppose you knew him,' said Dover grumpily, staring curiously at the vicar and wondering who he reminded him of.

'As far as anybody could,' agreed the vicar. He was a shortish, compact man with one of those square, bristly heads which were the hallmark of Prussian junkers before the First World War. When he had first come to the Beltour living there had been a movement amongst the older parishioners to nickname him 'The Gauleiter' but this had not caught on and the choirboys, on the grounds that his name was Liddle, had settled for calling him 'Box-top'. His humourous habit of sporting a rimless monocle on high days and holidays, while acknowledged to be somewhat bizarre, was generally approved. The inhabitants of Beltour were an old fashioned lot and expected their lords and their clergy to be different from the ordinary run of folk. 'I believe,' he went chatting on, 'that Marsh was a choirboy when he was younger, but that was before my time. He only started attending church on anything like a regular basis when he became engaged to that poor young woman, Charmian Tiffin. Of course, we've really got Arthur Tiffin to thank for that.' He broke off to enquire if they knew Arthur Tiffin.

'Oh, yes,' said MacGregor, hoping that the Reverend Mr Liddle didn't mind too much that Dover was now resting his aching feet on the little shelf provided for hymn books.

'Stout fellow, Arthur!' declared the vicar enthusiastically. 'A real pillar of the church – and of the village. We're lucky to have him. Got his early training in the army, you know. It always shows.'

The rain had slackened off to a heavy drizzle and the two tourists were summoning up their courage to leave. The vicar smiled wolfishly at them as they approached the door with its formidable array of begging boxes. Under the gaze of three interested pairs of eyes the man panicked and dropped one coin in the Church Fabric and yet another in Foreign Missions.

'God bless and God speed, dear friends!' called the vicar heartily and, in a profusion of muttered thanks, the tourists gratefully took their leave.

'Two fifty pence pieces!' said the vicar with understandable triumph. 'They made a quite unmistakable sound, you know.' He chuckled. 'Ah, well, it's more blessed to give than to receive, as we parsons always say! Now, what was it we were talking about?'

'You were telling us about Gary Marsh,' said MacGregor.

'Wrong!' laughed Mr Liddle whose natural high spirits were proof even against the pall of gloom Dover was endeavouring to cast over the proceedings. 'I was actually talking about Arthur Tiffin.' He leaned across and struck MacGregor a playful blow on the knee. 'You'll have to be sharper than that, sergeant, if you're going to get anywhere as a detective! Yes,' – he leaned back, making himself almost as much at home as Dover had been doing for the last ten minutes – 'salt of the earth, that chap! A born organizer! Of course The Royal South Shires Fusiliers was always a very good regiment. I did a couple of tours with them when I was a padre and I know what fine chaps they turned out. He practically runs Beltour House, you know, and I can't tell you what an asset he is to us here in the church. I was telling him so only the other day. "Give you a couple more years, Arthur," I said, "and you'll have the parish showing a profit!" '

Dover dug MacGregor in the ribs. 'Hasn't it stopped raining yet?'

'I'm afraid not, sir.'

Dover sighed heavily and eyed the vicar with more distaste than resignation while he thought of something rude to say. 'I should have thought you and Tiffin would have bored the pants off everybody with your reminiscences about the days when you were both playing soldiers.'

MacGregor cringed but Mr Liddle, in spite of his brutal Teutonic appearance, was inclined both by his nature and by his calling to see the best in almost everybody. 'Well, I might,' he admitted with a rueful grin. 'I enjoyed the army and I confess I do like talking about the good old days. But you can't accuse Arthur Tiffin of that. He never talks about his soldiering days and I respect him for it. He takes the view that he's a civilian now and there's no future in always harking back to the past. Funnily enough,' – and here even the vicar assumed that slightly smug expression which Beltour people acquired when they were about to introduce a certain name into the conversation – 'I was saying pretty much the same sort of thing to Lord Crouch only the other day. As a matter of fact, I even went so far as to compare Arthur with St Augustine of Hippo.'

MacGregor tried hard to look as though the comparison had some meaning for him. Dover didn't bother.

'Or,' said Mr Liddle helpfully, 'St Francis of Assissi.'

'Oh, quite!' said MacGregor confidently.

'Or even St Paul.'

'Ah,' said MacGregor with a smile.

Mr Liddle, however, was not the man to be bluffed by a member of the benighted laity. 'A conversion,' he explained. 'After a life more distinguished for high living than piety.'

'Of course,' agreed MacGregor, nodding his head while Dover picked up a hymn book and began leafing through it. 'You – er – think Mr Tiffin has had a bit of a past then, eh?'

The vicar shrugged his shoulders. 'I have sometimes wondered,' he admitted. 'Judging by the odd hint he's dropped, I don't think he was always a religious man. Few of us were, of course. Still,' – he grinned cheerfully – 'that's all water under the bridge now. Arthur is an outstanding church worker and a model to all of us, whatever he might have been in his youth. Frankly, I can't imagine what we should do here without him. He . . .'

Dover tossed his hymn book down with a loud bang. He'd got a sure fire method for shutting up people who seemed prepared to talk the hind leg off a donkey and he brought it into play now. 'Where,' he demanded abruptly, even pointing an accusing and nicotine-stained finger at the startled clergyman, 'were you at the time of the murder?'

Fifteen

For a split second Mr Liddle was tempted to treat the question as some sort of merry jape, but one look at Dover's scowling face was enough to make him revise his ideas pretty sharply. 'You can't be serious!' he protested. 'Where was I? Now, come on, my dear chap, you surely don't think that I had anything ...'

'You got something to hide?' asked Dover.

The vicar choked down his indignation. No doubt the fellow was only doing his duty but, even so, ... 'I can hardly tell you where I was at the time of the murder until you tell me what time the murder took place, can I?' he said with what he considered was commendable reasonableness.

Dover jerked his head knowingly at MacGregor. 'He's trying to be clever now!'

'Not at all!' objected the vicar.

'Garn!' scoffed Dover. 'If you don't know to the bloody minute when Marsh got rubbed out, you must be the only halfwit in the county who doesn't.'

Mr Liddle flushed and scraped one hand nervously over

the stubble on his head. 'I was in church,' he said coldly. 'Taking evensong.'

'Oh, I see!' sniggered Dover, anxious to display his ready wit. 'So there'd be no witnesses!'

This was a little too close to the truth for comfort. 'Of course there were witnesses!' retorted the vicar sharply. 'There are at least six people who can vouch for my presence here throughout the whole service, including Mr Tiffin. I should imagine his word would be good enough for anybody. He played the organ for us that evening and I would never be out of his sight from the first moment to the last. I preached a rather longer sermon than usual so for a good twenty minutes I was standing up there in that pulpit. If you think that left me with any opportunity to sneak out and murder Gary Marsh, you've got another think coming.'

Dover wasn't going to let old square-head off the hook as easily as that. 'Never mind the protests, mate!' he snarled. 'Let's be having some times.'

'The service began at six o'clock and finished at ten to seven, or a minute or two before.'

With this plain statement of fact Dover lost interest and MacGregor butted in to try and put the interview on a more business-like footing. 'Perhaps you could give me the names of those present, sir?'

'Of course.'

'Well, now, there's yourself and Mr Tiffin to start with.' MacGregor entered the names in his notebook. 'And the others, sir?'

Mr Liddle rattled off the distressingly short list of his evening congregation and pointed out a salient fact for Dover's especial benefit. 'I imagine that we all alibi each other, don't we?'

But Dover had already chucked the towel in. His grasshopper mind, ever unhealthily preoccupied with the delights of hanging, was now mulling over the problems likely to be posed by the vicar's neck. It was a very short, very strong and very muscular neck. It'd give any Jack Ketch one hell of a job, if topping hadn't been abolished and if this God-botherer here hadn't just successfully wriggled out of a murder charge.

'Sir?'

Reluctantly Dover broke off his ruminations about how you'd stop the hempen rope slipping up over the vicar's head because those little tightly set ears'd be no damned good. 'What?'

MacGregor put away his notebook. 'I was wondering if you had any further questions, sir?'

Dover sighed a dejected sigh, thought for a bit, remembered the cup of coffee he had promised himself for his morning's labours and dragged himself to his feet. MacGregor and the vicar stood up, too, and in silence watched Dover stump bad-temperedly out of the church.

MacGregor caught up with him by the lych gate, having done his best to restore the image of the Metropolitan Police in the eyes of the vicar. It is unlikely that he succeeded because a very stiff letter about police brutality appeared the following week in the *Church Times* under Mr Liddle's signature.

Dover got his coffee in the Ermyntrude Snack Bar and generously allowed MacGregor to stand him a couple of ham sandwiches as well. His generosity, however, did not extend to permitting further discussion of the case and MacGregor was shut up pretty smartly when he tried to bring up the question of the murder. Dover claimed that his brain needed a rest and, since there appeared to be no answer to this bland assertion, MacGregor drank his coffee in silence. When he had finished he gave Dover a cigarette and set off to walk back to Beltour Park to get the car. Dover remained in the snack bar and was soon snoozing gently over the table.

Not that Dover was asleep the whole time that MacGregor was away. On the contrary, the chief inspector stayed awake long enough to map out his activities for the whole of the afternoon. He'd have whatever muck it was Lady Priscilla served up for his lunch and then retire to his bedroom for a few hours of quiet and solitary thought. In a bit he'd get round to working out something useless for MacGregor to do.

In due course MacGregor deposited Dover at Beltour House and then made his own way to The Bull Reborn for his lunch. Dover moodily threaded his way through the groups of visitors and began clambering up those dratted stairs. All in all he was not displeased with his morning's labours. They were getting on, he told himself in between desperate gasps for breath, they were getting on. A few more suspects had been eliminated. . . . And what matter if they were . . . for the most part . . . the elderly and female members of Mr Liddle's congregation. . . . Thousands of murders . . . had probably . . . been committed . . . by elderly . . . and female . . . church . . . goers.

Lady Priscilla, looking harrassed, opened the door in response to Dover's kick. Lunch, she explained with grovelling apology, was not ready. Dover's face blackened immediately. He felt – and said – that this was inexcusable. He had long ago given up expecting his hostess to produce a decent meal but there was no reason why she shouldn't produce a prompt one.

Lady Priscilla bore the complaints with a stiff upper lip. 'My brother would like to see you right away,' she said.

'Your brother? I thought he was supposed to be in London.' Dover reflected, and not for the first time, that nobody ever told him anything.

'He's just got back. He said he must see you the moment you came in. That's why I've held lunch back.'

Dover's mouth settled into a discontented pout. 'What's he want?'

Lady Priscilla bit her lip, looked extremely worried and shook her head. 'I'm afraid I don't know. He's in the sitting room. I'll have your lunch ready the moment you've finished.'

Dover weakened sufficiently to ask a civil question. 'What is it?'

'Well, we're having a nettle and raddish salad but I've got you some chips and fish fingers from the deep freeze. The man at the village shop said they were frightfully good and very popular. I've read the cooking instructions most carefully and I don't think I shall have any problems.'

'I'll be there in five minutes,' said Dover. 'Or less. Don't forget the tomato ketchup! Oh, and I'll have a few rounds of bread and butter, while you're at it.'

Lord Crouch was standing by the window when Dover entered the sitting room. His Lordship had had ample time to prepare his opening remarks and blurted them out before Dover had even had time to sit down.

'I've got a confession to make!'

Dover could have hugged him. A confession! It was the break that every tenth rate, hopelessly bogged down detective prays for. Dover's face broke into a grin. This'd be one in the eye for MacGregor! Dover had claimed all along that it was old Crouch and, by God, he'd been right.

Still, gratitude was no excuse for not kicking a man when he was down. Dover composed his face into his best we-have-the-means-to-make-you-talk scowl. 'And about time, too!' he snarled. 'Why didn't you come clean at the beginning instead of putting me to all this bloody trouble?'

Lord Crouch drooped even more dejectedly and sighed. 'This may take some time,' he murmured.

'It'd better not!' retorted Dover. 'Look, I don't want your bleeding life story. A quick cough'll do me fine. Besides, my lunch'll be ready in a minute. Er – you got any cigarettes handy?'

'My sister and I don't indulge,' Lord Crouch reminded him timidly.

'Nothing to stop you keeping a few for your guests, is there?' muttered Dover crossly but he didn't pursue the matter. He had just recalled that there were some formalities to be observed. Blooming red tape, of course, but if you didn't watch your step these days you could bugger everything up. 'I've got to caution you,' he said with considerably more assurance than he felt. This was one of the many little details that he usually left to MacGregor. Still, needs must when the devil drives. He cleared his throat. 'Speak now,' he admonished an astonished Lord Crouch, 'or forever hold your peace!'

Lord Crouch blinked. 'Er – isn't that . . . isn't that part of the – er – marriage service, my dear fellow?'

Dover was furious. 'You trying to teach me my job?' he demanded.

'Good heavens, no!' Lord Crouch sagged even further by the curtains.

'Well, get on with it then!' growled Dover. 'Nothing long-winded, mind! Just a brief statement to the effect that you croaked What's-his-name, how you did it and why.'

Lord Crouch glanced across at Dover in an agony of indecision. One hesitated to contradict the dear chap, especially when he was an honoured guest under one's ancestral roof, but, on the other hand, one could hardly be expected to confess to a crime one hadn't committed just to oblige him. Lord Crouch sweated through his predicament and finally unlocked his jaws. 'I didn't – ah – actually murder Gary, don't you know.'

Dover swivelled his eyes up to the ceiling. 'Strewth, give him half a chance and this stuttering moron would stretch it out from now until tea-time! 'All right, all right!' he snapped. 'Have it your way. If you want to kid yourself it was manslaughter, that's fine by me. Just get on with it!'

Lord Crouch appeared to be trying to unscrew both of his hands at the wrists. This interview was turning out to be even more of a nightmare than he had envisaged. 'I had nothing to do with Gary's death at all!' he wailed in an unhappy splutter.

'Don't gimme that!' snarled Dover, glaring from screwed up, piggy eyes.

'But it's the truth!'

'Then what are we doing here, for God's sake?'

'I just wanted to tell you about the interview I had on the Sunday night with the poor boy, before he left to catch his train.'

Dover realized that it was a lost cause; he wasn't known as the Clinging Ivy of Scotland Yard for nothing. 'You quarrelled over something,' he prompted hopefully. 'And then you sneaked out into the darkness and bashed his head in.'

'No, no!' Lord Crouch beat himself on the temple in an effort to get the words out. 'It's just that I haven't been entirely honest and above-board with you about the subject of that interview.'

Dover sagged back sulkily in his chair. 'You can get twenty years for misleading the police,' he said.

'I have to admit that I was evasive.' Lord Crouch, a man of honour, made the acknowledgement painfully. 'At the time it seemed essential that I should be. It was important to other people, you see.'

'What other people?'

'My business associates,' croaked Lord Crouch. 'My business associates in the merger.'

'Oh, blimey!' groaned Dover. To think that he was having to wait for his lunch for this load of old codswallop. 'What bloody merger?'

'I think,' panted Lord Crouch, mopping his brow and collapsing into a chair, 'that I had better begin at the beginning.' There were few words better calculated to strike dismay into Dover's heart. 'You see, I have considerable business interests, quite apart from the running of Beltour. Actually, the house barely breaks even as a strictly commercial enterprise. The overheads are incredibly high. The herd of zebras alone . . .' Lord Crouch broke off and shook his head miserably as he thought of the herd of zebras. 'Well, I have for several years been connected with a large catering firm and recently we have been looking to expand and – er – diversify our interests. Take-overs and things, don't you know. Well, one of the concerns we had our eye on was the hotel in Dunningby in which Gary was currently working.'

The flicker of interest which twitched over Dover's face was faint, but it was there.

Vastly flattered and encouraged, Lord Crouch resumed his narrative with what was for him considerable animation. The fact that he had already written his story out and learnt it off by heart in the train was, of course, a great help and it was lucky for him that Dover didn't realize that one simple question could have wrecked the whole performance. 'You will understand how these things are done,' said Lord Crouch, baring his tomb-stone teeth in a shame-faced grin. 'The main point about take-overs, as I understand it, is secrecy. Once you let your victim get so much as a whiff of what's in the offing, the price goes up like a rocket.' On the train Lord Crouch hadn't cared much for the sound of the word 'victim' but he had been quite unable to think of an alternative. He was not, of course, a proper business man and had only become involved in city affairs because some companies still think a title on the board inspires confidence. 'So, you see, we had to be most frightfully careful. We had to find out as much as we could about this hotel – turnover, overheads, profit margins, visible and – er – invisible assets, staffing – and all without letting the present owners know of our interest.' Lord Crouch's long, hang-dog face split into another of his nervous grins. 'That's where Gary came in.'

'As a spy,' said Dover, who could always make the effort to be nasty.

'We called him our under-cover agent,' said Lord Crouch sadly. 'He was able, over a period of several months, to find out a great deal for us. When he came home on his free days

I used to arrange for him to call in at Beltour and report to me. Our chairman thought it better not to have anything in writing, don't you know. So, that's what Gary was doing here on the Sunday evening before he met his death.'

'And you reckon the owners of this hotel found out what he was up to and bumped him off?' Dover screwed up his nose doubtfully.

'Good heavens, no! Such an idea never crossed my mind. Besides, they didn't find out. We completed our take-over this morning and I can assure you that the whole business came as a complete shock to them.'

Dover put on a show of considerably more indignation than he felt. 'Why didn't you bloody well tell me all this before?' he demanded.

Lord Crouch gulped and sawed the air desperately with his hand for several seconds before he got his vocal chords functioning again. 'Our negotiations for the take-over had entered a most delicate and critical stage. One untoward word and the entire thing might have come crashing down about our ears. Like a pack of cards,' said Lord Crouch with a sudden burst of inspiration. 'I felt I owed it as a duty to my fellow directors, you see, to preserve a discreet silence.'

Dover's stomach rumbled loudly at this point but Lord Crouch had been nicely brought up and pretended not to notice. 'What was Marsh getting out of this?' asked Dover curiously.

'Marsh? Getting out of it?' Lord Crouch's attempt to stall for time was rather pathetic.

'Don't tell me he was doing all this snooping just for the sake of your big blue eyes!' sneered Dover. 'How big was the bribe?'

'Good gracious,' bleated Lord Crouch, 'there was no bribe! That would have been highly unethical.'

'But promising him the job of manager of your new motel wouldn't be, I suppose?' asked Dover, very sarcastic.

Lord Crouch went a painful red. 'There was no connection between the two transactions. Gary was a very – er – capable young man. He warranted the offer of such a position on his merits.'

'Ho, ho,' jeered Dover, 'now pull the other one! Here,' – he leaned forward and spoke to Lord Crouch as one man of the world to another – 'is it true that Marsh was your son?'

'Certainly not!' Lord Crouch spluttered furiously but he got the indignant denial out with admirable speed.

'That's what they say down in the village.'

Lord Crouch drew himself up stiffly. 'I am well aware of what they say down in the village, about both myself and my sister. They have been saying it for years and it is still nothing but scurrilous gossip. I am surprised that a man of your standing should give ear to it.'

Dover slumped back in his chair. 'You've always taken a great deal of interest in the lad,' he pointed out resentfully.

'My family has always taken a great deal of interest in the careers of any likely young people in the village. In Gary's case, we felt a double obligation. His aunt, Miss Marsh, has given us devoted and loyal service over many years and, then, the unfortunate circumstances of his birth . . .' Lord Crouch left the sentence unfinished and, after rather a long pause, began again. 'Besides . . .'

'Besides what?'

'Well, I have wondered from time to time whether one of our chaps might not have been responsible. For fathering Gary, I mean. Gary's mother would never apparently say anything about who his father was – she may well not have known for sure, of course – but my regiment was stationed up there at about that time. Henniford, where Gary's mother lived, is only a bicycle ride from Tuppeny Hill Camp, and you know what soldiers are.'

'Bloody young hooligans, most of 'em,' said Dover. 'This place you mentioned . . .'

'Henniford?'

'You know it?'

Lord Crouch squirmed unhappily. 'Well, I knew of it, of course, when I was serving in the Royal South Shires Fusiliers, but I never actually went there. There was a sort of unofficial rule, you see, at Tuppeny Hill Camp. Henniford was kind of out-of-bounds to officers. It was the preserve of the Other Ranks. When we wanted a drink or a bit of a night out, we used to go to a place called Cranleigh. That was several miles away in the other direction.'

Dover was frowning horribly. It might have been indigestion or even hunger, but it wasn't. Almost in spite of himself, a faint glimmer of light was trying to penetrate the murky recesses of his mind. 'There are other ex-soldiers from your regiment in this village, aren't there?'

'Of course. The South Shires is the county regiment. Round here has always been one of our best recruiting areas. And, naturally, when I have been engaging men for any position here at Beltour, I have always tried to give my ex-comrades priority. My own service career was, regrettably, very brief. My father's death, you remember. However, I always look back upon it as one of the happiest periods of my life. It's only natural that I should take an interest in the men who shared it with me, isn't it?'

Dover didn't bother answering. He was thinking. If he could just sort out one or two things, he was sure he'd get to the bottom of Marsh's murder – and wouldn't that make MacGregor sick! A few details to work out here and there – like who did it – and he'd be ready to spit right in his sergeant's eye. Dover didn't let his sudden burst of enthusiasm carry him away. All problems could well be postponed until after the inner man had been fortified.

Dover stood up. 'Time for lunch!' he said and waited impatiently for Lord Crouch to open the door for him.

Sixteen

Dover wasn't very good on the telephone, especially when the operator was a spirited lass who wasn't going to stand for that kind of foul language, no, not from nobody she wasn't. Dover reckoned his call was a matter of extreme urgency and he had only waited to have his lunch and a short period for digestion before rushing to the telephone to make it. The operator was unimpressed. Saying tartly that she sincerely hoped it *was* a matter of life and death, she pulled the plug out on him.

Dover screamed for assistance.

Lady Priscilla came at an extended trot. 'The Bull Reborn, chief inspector? Oh, but you can dial that direct. You don't need to bother the exchange.'

Not wishing to admit that his fingers were too fat to fit comfortably in the holes, Dover turned on the charm. 'When I need a lesson from you about how to use the bloody telephone,' he roared, 'I'll ask for it!'

A woman from a less deprived stratum of society would have promptly wrapped the telephone round Dover's thick head, but Lady Priscilla merely flinched and began meekly to dial the requisite number.

After an interminable delay of nearly thirty seconds, it appeared that Sergeant MacGregor was not available. He had gone out.

'Ask 'em where to!' hissed Dover, never one to bark himself.

Lady Priscilla asked. The Bull Reborn didn't know. Could they take a message?

'Bloody fool!' snarled Dover, conveniently forgetting that he himself had given MacGregor strict instructions to get lost for the afternoon. 'Trust him to go missing the minute you want him.'

'Perhaps the police in Claverhouse would know where he was,' suggested Lady Priscilla diffidently. 'Should I try them?'

'Suit yourself!' grunted Dover. 'Tell him I want to see him double-quick when you do get hold of him. And' – his appeal was more of a snarl than a supplication – 'try not to take all bloody day about it!'

Meanwhile, the object of all this trouble and ill will was bowling happily along the road on his way, as it happens, to Claverhouse. The relief of getting Dover's dead-weight off his back even for an hour or two was making MacGregor feel positively light-headed. So light-headed, in fact, that the sergeant was taking the supreme risk of pursuing his own line of enquiry, although he knew perfectly well that this was not what Dover had intended he should do with his free afternoon. So, MacGregor told himself cheerfully as he over-took yet another car, we shall just have to see that the old fool remains wallowing in his normal state of pig ignorance!

MacGregor, unlike his lord and master, had been giving considerable thought to the murder of Gary Marsh and had come to the conclusion that the murderer was not going to be found in Beltour. Dover had only been concentrating his attention on the village because it involved him in less effort than searching further afield, but MacGregor flattered himself that he was more than capable of embracing wider horizons. It was really the sinister and shadowy figure of Taffy O'Sullivan that had tempted MacGregor to strike out on his own. MacGregor, it must be appreciated, was a town dweller and, in spite of his police training, had some very romantic ideas about people who lived all the week in the country. In his heart of hearts he felt that they were really all pretty easy-going types, peasants who bickered amiably with their neighbours but who rarely, if ever, killed them. Townees, on the other hand, were quite different. Especially when they ran betting shops and had gangs of strong-arm men at their beck and call. No, the more MacGregor thought about it, the more attractive Claverhouse's underworld looked as the happy hunting ground for Gary Marsh's killer. Of course he'd no real evidence to back up his feeling but MacGregor, an unwilling pupil in the Dover school of detection, didn't bother to much about that.

He began his exploration of the seamier side of Claverhouse by calling at the police station. His reception was friendly enough on the surface, but it was only on the surface. Dover's methods had at first bewildered, and then outraged the local force and a rather icy politeness was now the order of the day. Everybody, from the chief constable down to the pimpliest cadet was intent on keeping well clear of those clowns they'd sent down from Scotland Yard.

'Taffy O'Sullivan?' queried Inspector Dawkins. 'Yes, I know him.'

'Officially?' MacGregor was concentrating so hard on appearing young, lean and keen that the question came out a mite more sharply than he had intended.

'No, not officially.' Inspector Dawkins was dying to know why the London jacks were suddenly taking an interest in Taffy O'Sullivan, but he would sooner have died than ask. 'He may run a couple of betting shops in our area, but we've not had any trouble from him. As far as we're concerned, he's as sober and upright a citizen as the next man.'

'Ah!' said MacGregor, now looking shrewd. He wished that Inspector Dawkins would be a trifle more inquisitive so that he could demonstrate that one member at least of the unholy partnership which had descended on Beltour wasn't an unmitigated slob.

Inspector Dawkins didn't weaken. 'Do you want his address?'

MacGregor, not to be outdone in stoicism, stifled his disappointment. 'If you've got it handy.'

'Well, his main office is just down the street from here. On the left hand side, just past what was the Bijou Bioscope Picture House.' Inspector Dawkins, over sensitive, realized that this might sound dafter than it actually was. 'It's a bingo hall now,' he explained, 'but you can still see it used to be a cinema. Mr O'Sullivan is usually there about this time of day.'

'Thanks!' MacGregor flashed his juvenile lead smile on the grounds that you never knew when you might need a friend. He gave Inspector Dawkins one last chance to relax. 'You busy?'

Inspector Dawkins was unrelenting. 'So, so,' he said and, rather pointedly, opened one of the pile of folders in front of him.

'Well,' – MacGregor's smile became a fraction less engaging – 'I mustn't keep you. There's no rest for any of us, is there?'

Inspector Dawkins let him get as far as the door. 'Oh,' he said, 'I almost forgot. Somebody rang up for you.'

'Rang up here?'

'Yes. It was all a bit confused but the sergeant on the desk gathered that your boss wanted to see you right away. Chief Inspector Rover.'

'Dover,' said MacGregor. He came back a few steps. 'They didn't say what he wanted?'

Inspector Dawkins shook his head.

'I say, do you think you could do me a favour?' The

smile was now ingratiating. 'If he rings up again, don't let on I called in here.'

'All right.'

Inspector Dawkins's manner was so distant that MacGregor felt obliged to explain further. 'It's just that I've got a couple of things to see to and I don't suppose he wants me for anything urgent.'

'No,' agreed Inspector Dawkins, careful to keep his voice quite expressionless, 'I don't suppose he does.'

Taffy O'Sullivan's betting shop wasn't hard to find and the disloyal thought crossed MacGregor's mind that even Dover might have stumbled across it without too much difficulty. The window was set out with three or four chipped and shabby model horses in illustration of the sport of kings and a string of down-trodden men passed continually in and out of the finger-smudged, glass plated doors. MacGregor slipped into the line and entered, ploughing his way through the discarded betting slips which carpeted the floor.

Inside the shop the mixture of tobacco smoke and sweaty socks got him by the throat and he made his way across to the counter trying to hold his breath. Behind a steel grill, somewhat like an enclosed nun in her parlour, sat a hard-faced young woman raking in the money with remarkably dirty hands. She chewed slowly and thoughtfully while MacGregor explained that he would like to speak to Mr O'Sullivan. When he'd finished the girl eyed him up and down and apparently decided he was harmless. She jerked her head towards the far end of the counter. MacGregor smiled his thanks – she was quite a nubile young woman – and, following the inclination of her head, made his way behind the counter and into a tiny office at the back.

'Mr Taffy O'Sullivan?'

The man working away at the untidy roll top desk turned round. 'Sure is, boss!' he grinned and leaned back to enjoy the look on MacGregor's face.

Whatever else MacGregor had been expecting, he had not been expecting to find that Taffy O'Sullivan was a huge, amiable and very black West Indian. Trying to hide his surprise, he began to introduce himself but the massive negro flapped him into silence with a lordly wave of his enormous, pink-palmed hand.

'You're the fuzz, man!' he announced. 'And I sure don't need anybody to tell me that. What's taken you so long?'

'You've been expecting us?' MacGregor frowned.

'Sure have. Soon as I heard somebody'd pushed that Marsh cat through dem pearly gates, I knew you pigs'd be snuffling around. I told 'em out there to be sure and show you right in. Mind you,'—Taffy O'Sullivan made the admission with disarming frankness—'I did reckon it'd be the old boar that'd come a-knocking at my door. How come they've only sent me a little piglet, huh?'

The body-wobbling chuckles which accompanied this question were meant to take some of the sting out of it, but MacGregor was not amused. He glared at Mr O'Sullivan with a bleak sourness of which Dover himself would not have been too ashamed. 'You knew Gary Marsh?'

'You know I did, man! And I know all about Josh's little old chinwag with you boys at The White Feathers.'

'Marsh owed you money?'

Taffy O'Sullivan shook his head slowly in mock self-reproach. 'I *will* let these trashy white boys bet on credit. It'll be the ruin of me.'

'And you wanted him to settle up?'

'I sure did!' agreed Taffy O'Sullivan with unshak-able good humour. His accent wandered uncertainly between black-faced minstrel and Wolverhampton, but his affability never wavered.

'And for gambling debts you have no redress in law.'

'Sure haven't!' said Taffy with a laugh. 'The courts is closed to the likes of me.'

'So you resort to strong-arm methods?'

Taffy O'Sullivan almost fell out of his chair. 'I told 'em that's what you'd say!' he roared, wiping the tears of mirth from his eyes. 'You cats is sure predictable. They issue you with little old gramophone records or something?'

MacGregor had a sneaking feeling that the interview was slipping out of his control. 'Where were you the night Marsh was killed?' he barked.

Taffy O'Sullivan laughed so much this time that he could hardly speak. 'I've got six alibis lined up, piglet!' he gasped. 'Which one would you like, huh? They'll all stand up in court, that I can guarantee!'

'I've a bloody good mind to run you in!' snarled MacGregor, stripping off the kid gloves with a vengeance.

'You'll need help, brother!' warned Taffy O'Sullivan with a grin.

The implied insult both to his muscles and his manhood cut MacGregor to the quick, but he took another look at the powerful figure confronting him and wisely confined himself to verbal onslaughts. 'You'll not get away with this, O'Sullivan!'

'Now, stop leaning on me, boy! Use them old brains of yours! I'm a peaceful character. You go and ask the local bluebottles.'

'I already have,' said MacGregor grimly.

For the first time Taffy O'Sullivan looked disconcerted. 'You have?' he asked. 'Well, there's a thing, now!' He whistled softly to himself and gazed up at the ceiling. 'It seems I have been casting my bread on some very ungrateful waters. Or are they so stupid they don't know now how to use a telephone? Still,' – philosophically he pushed the problems of bribery and corruption to one side – 'go and have another word with them. They'll tell you I'm not the sort of gentleman to risk fifteen years in pokey for a lousy old twenty pounds.'

'Forty!' said MacGregor.

'It's still peanuts, man!'

'You might want to encourage the others.'

Taffy O'Sullivan nodded his agreement and his under-standing. 'Oh, sure. One sign of weakness in my line of business and they're crawling all over you, the twisting bastards! But give me credit for some basic common sense, man! If I was a-going to rub Marsh out, I wouldn't have done it myself, now would I? And I wouldn't have let any of my gallant band of assistants get involved, either. I'm not that stupid. Jesus, man, I'd have hired me a London boy to do me a real professional job. A gun or a knife. You can get likely lads for that two-a-penny up in the Smoke.'

MacGregor couldn't help but recognize the force of this argument. No crook worth his salt these days settled his own accounts. It was the age of specialization in crime as in everything else. MacGregor also knew that he was getting precisely nowhere in his eyeball to eyeball confrontation with Mr O'Sullivan and he began to search anxiously for some means of breaking off the engagement without too much loss of face. He was saved by the bell.

Taffy O'Sullivan's large black hand engulfed the tele-phone receiver. After a few unrevealing words he looked across at MacGregor. 'It's the local pigs, man. Is your handle MacGregor?'

'Yes.'

'You know a cat called Dover?'

MacGregor sadly acknowledged that he did.

Taffy O'Sullivan dropped the receiver back on its rest and jerked his head towards the door. 'He's whistling, boy!'

When MacGregor got back to Beltour, he found Dover not so much whistling as steaming.

'Where the hell have you been?' The chief inspector was reclining on the top of his bed and looking decidedly lumpish.

MacGregor nerved himself to offer a diplomatic, if totally unrevealing, account of his whereabouts and activities, but Dover didn't really want to know.

'You can tell me later!' he snapped. 'I've solved the bloody case, anyhow. It's a good thing there's one of us who doesn't sit around on his backside all day trying to look pretty!'

'Yes, sir,' said MacGregor. 'Er – who do you think the murderer is, sir?' With great restraint he didn't add the words 'this time' to his question.

Dover's never very sunny face clouded over. ' 'Strewth, I haven't got that far!' he objected. 'Trust you to want the whole thing handed to you on a bloody plate. I've just worked out the general principle of the thing. It's up to you to sort out the flipping details.'

MacGregor chided himself for ever having thought otherwise. 'I see, sir,' he said patiently.

One day, Dover promised himself, when he didn't feel so fagged, he'd punch that smug, superior face into an un-recognizable pulp. 'Did you know that Henniford was within spitting distance of Tuppeny Hill Camp?'

MacGregor shook his head. 'No, sir,' he admitted. 'Er – does it matter?'

Dover was impatient to get things over and done with so he ignored this piece of impertinence for the moment. 'Of course it matters, you moron! Henniford is the dump where Marsh's mother was living when he was born and Tuppeny Hill Camp is where Lord Crouch's bunch of little tin soldiers was stationed.'

'Really, sir?' MacGregor suppressed a sigh. They couldn't – surely – be back at poor Lord Crouch again, could they?

Dover knew exactly what MacGregor was thinking, and resented it. 'I reckon Marsh's mother was the regimental sweetheart. And obliging with it.'

'Ah!' MacGregor received Dover's wilder speculations coolly.

'Do you know how many men in this village served in that regiment?'

MacGregor saw which way Dover's thoughts – for want of a better word – were wending and sighed audibly this time.

'The Royal South Shires Fusiliers, sir? Oh, quite a number, I should imagine. I gather it mainly recruits in these parts. Well, there's Lord Crouch, himself, of course, and the landlord of The Bull Reborn. The vicar, too. Didn't he say he was attached to the South Shires at some time or another? I don't know whether he was with them at the time of Marsh's conception.'

'So, that's what you've got to find out, isn't it?' Dover was now paying more attention to the plumping up of his pillows. He wondered whether it was worth the effort of getting off the bed so that he could get the eiderdown free to pull over him.

'Your theory, sir, is that one of the ex-soldiers in the village is Marsh's father?' said MacGregor slowly. He was thinking hard. Sometimes, the law of averages being what it is, even Dover hit on the truth. 'But, supposing that he is, what difference does it make? It doesn't mean that he murdered Marsh. I mean, what would his motive be? Fear of exposure?'

'Could be,' grunted Dover as he settled down. The eiderdown wasn't worth the trouble.

'It's a bit thin, isn't it, sir?' MacGregor shook his head doubtfully. Suddenly he looked up. 'That stroppy little snout of yours, sir! Josh! He's an ex-fusilier, too!'

Dover lifted his head a quarter of an inch from the pillow. 'How do you know that?'

'He was wearing a badge in his lapel, sir. One of those old comrades' association things. I remember wondering vaguely how on earth a misbegotten runt like that ever got accepted into the army. The South Shires Fusiliers,' said MacGregor, remembering Lord Crouch, 'must be a pretty crummy bunch.'

'Uh,' said Dover sleepily. He brightened up a bit. 'I wouldn't mind pinning it on that little rat. You'd better have a good look at him while you're at it.'

MacGregor nodded his head absently. He'd more

important things on his mind just at that moment than exchanging idle chit-chat with Dover. There was somebody else. Sometime somebody had just casually mentioned....

'Arthur Tiffin!' gasped MacGregor.

Dover came out of the arms of Morpheus with an almost audible pop. *'Arthur Tiffin?'*

MacGregor, shaken by his own brilliance, sat down on the edge of the bed. 'Arthur Tiffin was in the South Shires, sir. Don't you remember? His wife told us.' MacGregor smacked himself across the forehead in a gesture of self reproach. 'She told us he'd actually been Lord Crouch's batman. You see what that means, don't you, sir? That would almost certainly put him in Tuppeny Hill Camp at the relevant time because Lord Crouch's military career was a pretty short one and I don't think he was ever stationed anywhere else. And, by golly,' – MacGregor stared at Dover – 'Arthur Tiffin would have an absolutely first class motive for murdering Marsh, wouldn't he?'

Dover struggled into a sitting position as some of MacGregor's excitement got through to him. 'Wouldn't he?' he asked, trying to blink the sleep out of his eyes.

'Of course, sir!' There was nothing MacGregor enjoyed more than explaining the painfully obvious to Dover. 'Gary Marsh was going to marry Charmian Tiffin, Arthur Tiffin's daughter. They were half-brother and sister, for God's sake!'

'Oh.' Dover was disconcerted by the speed with which MacGregor was advancing and decided it was about time he started picking holes in a theory which, with a modicum of decent luck, he might have thought of first. 'No,' he said, 'that can't be right.'

'Why not?'

'Because everybody says Tiffin and his missus were breaking their necks to get that girl off their hands, that's why. They practically shanghaied Marsh. Tiffin would hardly have gone to those lengths if the lad had been his blooming bastard, would he? He'd have busted a gut trying to stop 'em. And it wouldn't have been difficult because, by all accounts, Marsh wasn't overkeen in the first place.'

MacGregor hesitated only for a second before his brain, now ticking over like a well-tuned computer, rattled out the answer. 'Ah, but he didn't know, sir!'

'Says who?'

'The landlord of The Bull Reborn, sir!'

Dover had an awful suspicion that he was being left behind in the race. 'The landlord of the Bull Reborn?' he repeated.

'Don't you remember, sir?' To Dover's astonishment, and alarm, MacGregor edged further up the bed. 'The landlord told us that, when they called in the pub for a drink on the Sunday afternoon, Marsh and Arthur Tiffin were talking about Henniford and Tuppeny Hill Camp. The landlord only registered the names at all because he'd been up there himself when he was a soldier. Now, at the time, I assumed – and I expect you did too, sir' – MacGregor put it kindly – 'that this was just Arthur Tiffin boring the pants off the younger man with stories about his military career. But, you recall what both the vicar and Mrs Tiffin told us, sir!'

Dover duly nodded his head and tried to look as though he did.

MacGregor wasn't fooled and, in any case, he had no intention of not continuing his masterly exposition. 'They both said that Arthur Tiffin never talked about his time as a soldier. Never. So, if he and Marsh were talking about Henniford and Tuppeny Hill Camp, it's a fair bet that it was Marsh who introduced them into the conversation. He was probably telling Tiffin about the circumstances surrounding his birth. You remember Mrs Tiffin said that that was what the interview was supposed to be about.'

Dover had been trying to shove a word in edgeways for

some time and now he managed it. 'So, for the first time, Tiffin realizes that he must be Marsh's father!'

MacGregor filled his lungs and snatched the conversation back again. 'Or, at least, that there was a good chance he might be. Even that would be enough to make him act.'

' 'Strewth,' said Dover, with some admiration, 'he didn't waste much blooming time, did he?'

'He probably realized that he might never get a better opportunity. He'd know all about Marsh going to catch his train along that deserted path through Bluebell Wood and, besides, he simply daren't take the risk of waiting. The longer he let the engagement go on, the worse things might get. I mean, I know that neither Gary Marsh nor Charmian Tiffin seem to have been the wildly passionate type but – well – you never know, do you?'

Dover chewed his bottom lip. 'Why didn't Tiffin just tell Marsh?'

'Oh, there are a dozen reasons, sir!' MacGregor's cockiness was beginning to get on Dover's wick. 'For one thing, Marsh might have been a bit kinky and not minded marrying his half sister.'

'Oh, blimey!' groaned Dover.

'Well, actually, sir, I think it's far more likely that Tiffin just couldn't face all the family complications a broken engagement would cause. You can imagine what Mrs Tiffin would have to say about it. She'd make his life a hell on earth.'

'You can say that again,' said Dover gloomily. He was a married man himself and knew what he was talking about. ' 'Course, he might have been able to persuade Marsh to keep his mouth shut.'

'And be held responsible for breaking off the engagement, sir? In a small village like this? He'd have had to flee the country.'

'I suppose so,' sighed Dover. 'No, I reckon Tiffin took

the only way out. That way, he saves his reputation, keeps his wife off his back and stops a misalliance. I don't know that in those circumstances I wouldn't have committed murder myself.' He looked up as MacGregor jumped to his feet. 'Where are you going?'

'Don't you think we'd better go and see Tiffin right away, sir?'

'I suppose so,' said Dover reluctantly. Privately, he thought Arthur Tiffin could well keep until morning but he suspected that, now MacGregor was hot on the trail, there was going to be no holding him. If Dover didn't get a move on, that young whelp would be off, nabbing Arthur Tiffin and all the glory for himself. 'Now?' he asked. 'Oh, well, in that case, stop standing there like a bloody lemon on a monument! Make yourself useful! Shove my boots over!'

MacGregor put Dover's boots on for him. It was quicker that way though close proximity to Dover's feet was not to be recommended to those with weak stomachs and sensitive noses.

Dover watched sullenly while MacGregor struggled with the laces. 'Tell you one thing,' he said in his least enthusiastic voice.

'Sir?'

'You haven't got a scrap of bloody evidence.'

MacGregor finished untangling the bits of chewed string with which Dover apparently kept his boots on. 'I think he'll crack all right, sir, once we face him with the facts.'

'Always the bloody optimist!' sneered Dover as he stood up and took a tentative step or two to test that MacGregor had done his work properly. 'Coat!' he ordered.

MacGregor trotted off to collect Dover's overcoat from where Lady Priscilla had carefully hung it behind the door.

'Tiffin's no fool,' warned Dover with a sniff. 'And he's probably not as soft as he looks. Still,' – he let MacGregor manoeuvre his left arm into the left sleeve – 'Not to worry, laddie! I'll soon get a confession out of him for you. A couple of thumps in the kidneys and my boot across his shins and he'll be spewing his guts up. There'll not be a mark on him, either,' added Dover proudly. 'Well, not where it shows.' He grinned evilly and glanced round the room. 'Hat!'

Seventeen

Dover had actually reached the door before he remembered that he was the type of man who prided himself on using his head to save his legs. He stopped abruptly. MacGregor, who'd thought they were really going places this time, cannoned softly into him.

'Hey, watch it!' growled Dover, choosing to behave as though MacGregor was on the point of making an improper approach to him.

MacGregor clenched his fists. One day.... 'Have you forgotten something, sir?' he asked as calmly as he could.

'Why should I go chasing all over after a blooming murderer?' demanded Dover indignantly. 'Up and down those flaming stairs like a yo-yo? Besides, it'll be crawling with trippers down there and we don't want an audience, do we?' He executed a sloppy about turn and began to retrace what few steps he'd taken.

MacGregor remained hovering by the door like a fish out of water. Who but Dover, of course, would ever dream of arresting a man for murder in his own bedroom? 'Do you want me to go and fetch him, sir?'

'Save your energy, laddie!' said Dover, feeling quite

generous now that he was sitting down again. 'Tell Lady What's-her-name to give him a ring on that house phone of theirs.'

MacGregor didn't care for the idea of asking someone of Lady Priscilla's birth and position to perform such a menial task. 'Oh, it's no trouble, sir. It won't take me a minute just to pop ...'

Dover didn't like people arguing with him. 'Tell Lady P to ring for him!' he snarled and, taking off his bowler hat, flung it petulantly on the bed.

Lady Priscilla was in the kitchen, up to her eyebrows in soya bean flour and peering very anxiously at a recipe book which she'd got propped up against a jar of fermenting home-made jam. She received the request and MacGregor's fulsome apologies with a harrassed smile.

'Oh, no, it's no trouble at all, sergeant,' she said. 'I'll just wash my hands and ... Mr Dover wants to see him right away, does he?'

'The sooner the better,' said MacGregor, looking very important about it. 'It's a matter of extreme urgency, otherwise' – and here Lady Priscilla got the youthful knight-errant smile – 'we would never have asked for your assistance.'

Lady Priscilla fluttered with delight and MacGregor took a light dusting of soya bean flour back to Dover's bedroom.

Half an hour later, the two detectives were still sitting there.

'That bloody woman!' howled Dover. 'What does she think she's playing at?'

MacGregor went to find out.

'Lady Priscilla telephoned Tiffin almost immediately, sir,' he reported a moment or two later. 'She told him we wanted to see him right away. We've just rung down again and the woman on the souvenir stall says he left some time ago.'

'Left?' Dover's face was not a pretty sight.

'The house, sir.'

'Damn and blast it!' exploded Dover. 'He's made a run for it! And it's all your bloody fault, MacGregor! If it'd been left to me we'd have gone downstairs and nabbed him before he knew what hit him.'

'Yes, sir.' MacGregor knew the futility of arguing.

'Well, you'd better get cracking and organize a search, then!' Dover began to remove his overcoat. 'Alert the local police, set up road blocks, send out patrols. Not that it'll do any blooming good. He'll be out of the country by now.' He looked up impatiently. 'Well, what are you waiting for?'

'I was just wondering, sir.'

'Oh, put the flags out!' sneered Dover, trying to push his right boot off without untying the laces. 'You've done enough wondering for one day, laddie, and look where it's landed us.'

'Tiffin may have gone home, sir.'

'And pigs might fly!'

'If he is going to make a run for it, sir, he'll need money, a passport, a change of clothing.'

Dover could see what was coming. 'He's probably been keeping a suitcase already packed hidden away somewhere,' he grumbled.

'No, I don't think so, sir. The lady on the souvenir stall who saw him go said he wasn't carrying anything. It's worth a try, isn't it, sir?'

There's none as dense as those who don't want to know. 'What is?'

'Us going round to his house, sir. I think there's a fair chance that that's where he's gone.'

Dover sighed. It was like being on a bloody treadmill. 'Oh, well, get the car then!' he growled.

The Tiffins' cottage was looking as normal as it was ever likely to do when MacGregor brought the car to a halt outside the gate.

'He's here, sir! I was right!'

Dover was still trying to extract himself from the car. 'How do you know?'

'His bicycle's there, sir.'

' 'Strewth!' muttered Dover. 'Bloody Sherlock Holmes now!'

It was Mrs Tiffin who opened the door. 'Well, seems you two just can't keep away!' she greeted them cheerfully. She gave MacGregor a very special smile. 'Charmian'll be back any minute. You won't have long to wait. Well,' – she extended her smile to include Dover – 'I suppose I'd better go and put the kettle on.'

MacGregor had scruples about sitting down and sharing a high tea with a man he was about to arrest for murder. 'Is your husband in?' he asked.

'Up in the bathroom, dear,' said Mrs Tiffin with an exasperated jerk of her head. 'As usual.' She turned her attention back to Dover. 'Think you could manage a bit of my toad-in-the-hole?'

Dover was not to be outdone in the matter of friendly exchanges. 'I could manage,' he responded gallantly as he waddled across the threshold, 'a lot!'

Mrs Tiffin let rip a delighted shriek at such bare-faced sauciness and sped away in the direction of her kitchen while somewhere, up above their heads, a cistern emptied and filled itself with much satisfied gurgling. A few seconds later and Mr Tiffin came down the stairs.

'Oh, there you are!' he said, leading the way into the sitting room. 'I got your message.'

Dover sat himself down at the table and grabbed a couple of slices of bread and butter just to keep body and soul together. 'What message?'

'About you wanting to see me,' explained Mr Tiffin as he took the chair opposite. 'I was beginning to wonder where you'd got to.'

MacGregor, for what it was worth, studiously refrained from making himself at home. 'We wanted to see you in the flat at Beltour,' he pointed out sternly.

Mr Tiffin reached for a piece of bread and butter while

there was still some left. 'Really? Well, that's Lady Priscilla all over, you know. If you want something mucked up, give it to her to do. Still,' – he began to pour the milk in the cups – 'what's on your mind?'

'We've come to arrest you for the murder of Gary Marsh,' said Dover. The remark was intended not so much to shock Mr Tiffin into a full and frank confession as to put him off his food, but it failed on both counts.

Mr Tiffin calmly took another piece of bread and butter. 'They really ought to have you on the telly!' he chuckled. 'The way you said that! Face as straight as an undertaker's and everything!'

Dover had a crushing retort trembling on his lip but Mrs Tiffin's triumphant entry with two plates heaped high with toad-in-the-hole effectively diverted his mind to higher things.

Mr Tiffin, though, wanted his better half to share the fun. 'What do you think, Alice? Mr Dover here thinks I killed poor Gary! First our Charmian, now me. You'd better look out, love, or it'll be your turn next!'

Mrs Tiffin glared at her husband, and at Dover. 'It's a pity some people haven't got a sense of decency!' she snapped. 'I don't think the death of our Charmian's fiancé is anything to make silly jokes about.'

'I'm afraid it's not a joke, Mrs Tiffin.' MacGregor was still standing just inside the door. No-one knew better than he did that this was no way to go about confronting a criminal with his misdeeds, but there was nothing like a few years of close association with Dover to make you lower your standards. 'We have good grounds for believing that your husband was responsible for Marsh's death.'

'Well, you've got a blooming nerve, I must say!' Mrs Tiffin's eyes flashed and she clamped both hands resolutely on her hips. 'Of all the cheek! Coming here and.... Why, I've a good mind to put my hat and coat on this minute and go round and see what Lord Crouch's got to say about all this. He'll soon take the wind out of your sails, young man! He'll . . .'

'Keep your hair on, love,' advised Mr Tiffin placidly. 'It's just some misunderstanding, that's all.'

'Misunderstanding be blowed!' spluttered Dover, digging another sausage out of its delicious hole. 'You murdered Gary Marsh and, soon as I've had my second cup of tea, I'm going to run you in for it.' He transferred his gaze to Mrs Tiffin. 'Three lumps this time, missus!'

But Mrs Tiffin was really annoyed. She folded her arms. 'Pour your own out!' she responded tartly. 'I'm not raising another finger for you until we've got to the bottom of this nonsense.'

MacGregor sighed. With Dover's mouth stuffed full of the best home cooking for fifty miles around, it was clearly up to him. 'We have evidence, Mrs Tiffin,' he began, gilding the lily a little because there was no point in admitting that it was just one of the wilder ideas thrown off the top of Dover's head, 'that your husband was Gary Marsh's father. Gary Marsh, as you may know, was born – or at any rate conceived – in the village of Henniford. At the relevant time, your husband was stationed near by at the army camp at Tuppeny Hill.'

'Along with a couple of hundred other able-bodied, red-blooded men!' put in Mr Tiffin quickly with a side ways glance at his wife's rapidly hardening face.

MacGregor ignored the interruption. 'Of course your husband was unaware of this relationship. He only found out about it during that conversation he had with Gary Marsh last Sunday in the bar of The Bull Reborn. You yourself, Mrs Tiffin, remarked that your husband was not himself when he came home that afternoon. No wonder. He had suddenly realized what a dreadful predicament he was in. This young man, his own son, was about to get married to Charmian, his own daughter. It was unthinkable. Somehow he had to stop it.'

'Lies!' objected Mr Tiffin, wilting visibly as his wife turned to look at him. 'A pack of lies!'

'Hold your tongue, you filthy pig!' spat Mrs Tiffin. She switched her attention back to MacGregor. 'Go on!' she instructed grimly.

'Well, that's about all there is, Mrs Tiffin. Your husband obviously felt that he couldn't reveal the true facts of the situation. That would have meant admitting to you, to your daughter and to the world at large that he had been unfaithful to his marriage vows twenty years and more ago. I suppose he just felt he couldn't do it, not with him being such a pillar of the church and everything. That left him with only one solution. To stop the marriage, he had to kill Gary Marsh.'

MacGregor thought he had summarized the case against Arthur Tiffin rather well. Mrs Tiffin thought so, too. She had already found her husband guilty without any extenuating circumstances and was now about to carry out the sentence.

Mr Tiffin made a pathetic attempt to avert the wrath to come. 'Here, steady on, Alice!' he begged. 'You don't believe all this rubbish, do you?'

Mrs Tiffin continued her progress towards the poker. 'I believe every word!' she stated uncompromisingly. 'Every word! Because I know you, Arthur Tiffin. With your dirty mind and your unspeakable lusts. You've always been sex mad.' She picked up the poker. 'I'm just surprised you've only got one bastard to your name.'

'Hey, watch it dear!' Mr Tiffin got up from his seat at the table and appealed to MacGregor. 'I want protection. This is all your fault. The least you can do is keep her off till she's simmered down a bit.'

'Give us a confession,' said Dover, dropping his knife and fork on to a locust clean plate, 'and we'll have you locked up in a nice safe cell in no time. She won't be able to get at you there.'

Mr Tiffin began an unobtrusive retreat round the room. 'Confess? Not flipping likely! I deny the whole thing. Categorically. You haven't an atom of proof. And, even if I was Gary Marsh's father,' – he swung a chair across Mrs Tiffin's path – 'which I most definitely am not, that still doesn't mean I murdered him. I've got an alibi. I was in church. You ask the vicar and all the rest of the congregation.'

'Hanging's too good for you!' announced Mrs Tiffin, doggedly tracking her husband through the tables and chairs. 'I don't want you dead, Arthur. I want you alive and suffering. It'll be some small consolation for what you've put me and our Charmian through all these years. The shame you've brought on us!'

'Keep her off!' pleaded Mr Tiffin.

'Tell us the truth, then,' advised Dover, making a devastating start on the home-baked plum cake. 'We've got you bang to rights but a confession always goes down well with the judge.'

'I didn't do it!' insisted Mr Tiffin, beginning to find the sitting room a little short on cover. 'I've got a cast-iron alibi. Why don't you bloody well listen?'

Mrs Tiffin permitted herself a frisson of triumph. 'Foul language now, is it?' she demanded. 'Oh, we're seeing you in your true colours and no mistake. Are there no depths to which you won't sink, you animal?'

MacGregor, seeing that Mr Tiffin had got himself holed up by the window, abandoned his post by the door and ventured a word in Dover's ear. 'I think we ought to take him off to the station, sir.'

Dover ground his way moodily through the last slice of cake. 'Pity you didn't think about that bloody alibi before dragging me down here on a wild goose chase,' he grumbled.

'Oh, I'm sure we can break that down, sir.'

Dover ran an exploratory tongue round his upper set. 'He seems pretty confident.'

'Bluff, sir.'

'The vicar and a bunch of God botherers? You'll have a hell of a job convincing a jury that they're party to a fiddle.'

MacGregor did not fail to notice that the foolhardy decision to arrest Arthur Tiffin was now being firmly accredited to him. Oh, well, it was no good arguing about it. 'I still think we should take the risk, sir.'

'And get hauled over the coals for false arrest?' yelped Dover indignantly. He was cheesed off to the back teeth with the whole tedious business and thought righteous indignation was a rather novel way of sliding out from under. 'I happen to have a reputation to think of, laddie, even if you haven't.'

MacGregor shrugged his shoulders and prepared to chalk up yet another dreary failure. 'Well, in that case, sir, I suppose we'd just better cut our losses and leave.' He watched Mr and Mrs Tiffin as they continued their intricate manoeuvrings round the room. 'At least we'll be sure that Tiffin isn't going to get away with it scot free.'

Dover examined the tea table and satisfied himself that nothing edible had been overlooked. He hoisted himself wearily to his feet. 'We'll pop in and see that fool of a Chief Constable before we go back to London and tell him that Tiffin's the murderer,' he said, apparently anxious to assure his sergeant that they weren't just going to walk away and do nothing. 'He'll spread the word around. Tiffin's life' – he paused while the subject of his concern flashed past in a vain attempt to reach the kitchen door – 'won't be worth living. Cheer up, MacGregor,' he added comfortably as he got under way, 'you can't win 'em all.'

MacGregor followed his lord and master out of the cottage and carefully closed the front door on the sounds of strife which were already breaking out in the sitting room. He looked up to find that Dover was nose to nose with a little old lady who was blocking his way down the garden path.

'What's she doing here?' demanded Dover.

MacGregor, not surprisingly, didn't know.

'Well, ask her, you damned fool!'

'Oh, I was only coming to see Mrs Tiffin,' said the little old lady. She glanced at the bicycle propped up against the wall. 'I hadn't realized that Mr Tiffin was at home. I'll call some other time.'

'Watchergothere?' demanded Dover, determined to take his frustration out on somebody – and who better than a little old lady?

'Nothing!' The little old lady clutched the small parcel she was carrying even closer and went a bright red. 'Er – nothing at all.'

She attempted to withdraw but Dover yanked her back. 'Don't gimme that!' he snarled.

'It's only a present,' squeaked the little old lady. 'For Mrs Tiffin. Well, for Mr Tiffin, actually, but of course I couldn't possibly give it to him.'

'Why not?' Dover looked at the parcel with interest. A pot of home made jam, perhaps? Or honey?

'Oh, I just couldn't!' repeated the little old lady faintly. 'I'd die with embarrassment.'

Dover took time off to toss his considered opinion over his shoulder to MacGregor. 'We've got a right nutter here!' He swung back to his, as he hoped, helpless victim. 'Look, I'm a police officer and I want to know what's in that parcel. What's your name, anyhow?'

'Sampson. Miss Sampson.'

It meant Sweet Fanny Adams to Dover, of course, who'd difficulty knowing what day of the week it was, but MacGregor was quick to pick it up. 'Oh, yes,' he said. 'You're a member of Mr Liddle's congregation, aren't you?'

Miss Sampson, grateful for being addressed as though she was a human being, shyly admitted that she was.

'Well,' said MacGregor kindly, 'if you'll just tell us what's in the parcel, I'm sure we needn't detain you any longer.'

Miss Sampson was not one to stand on her rights. Indeed,

she was quite willing to help such a nice young man. 'It's some medicine.'

'Medicine?'

'A herbal remedy, of course. From my own recipe. Everyone says it is most efficacious and I'm sure it will clear up Mr Tiffin's little complaint in no time. I would have brought it round first thing on Monday morning, of course, but I found I had run out of supplies and it takes several days, you understand, to brew up a fresh quantity from scratch. It all has to be infused, you know, and then articum lappa is not at all easy to come by these days.'

'Mr Tiffin's complaint? And what's that when it's at home?'

Miss Sampson flinched pitifully at finding herself once more the object of Dover's attention and swallowed hard. 'Well, it's his – er – bladder, I believe,' she whispered.

'Oh, Jesus!' groaned Dover.

Miss Sampson turned back to MacGregor. 'Poor man, I felt so terribly embarrassed for him on Sunday night. I mean, fancy having to slip out right in the middle of Evensong! He was away such a long time, too, and he looked so simply dreadful when he crept back in again. He must have been in agony. I . . .'

'Just a minute!' There were some things so obvious that even Dover could see them. 'Are you saying that Arthur Tiffin sneaked out of church?'

Miss Sampson blinked at the vehemence with which the question was fired at her. 'That's right.'

'Last Sunday night?'

'Yes.'

'How long was he gone?'

'Oh, ten minutes. A quarter of an hour, perhaps. He missed most of dear Mr Liddle's most excellent sermon, I'm afraid.

' 'Strewth!' Dover's face broke into an evil grin. 'Go get him, laddie!'

MacGregor was less impetuous. 'Oh, but don't you think, sir, that we ought to ... ?'

'What are you belly-aching about now?' demanded Dover furiously. 'That's Tiffin's alibi busted wide open! You gone deaf or something? This old biddy here has put the kibosh right on him.'

'But – don't you remember, sir? – Mr Liddle said he was present throughout the entire service. If Miss Sampson saw him leave, why didn't the Vicar? Or anybody else, for that matter?'

'Trust you to start nit-picking!' snarled Dover before letting fly with another blast in Miss Sampson's direction. 'Well?'

'Well, – er – what?'

'You heard the bloody question!'

'Oh, I see.' Miss Sampson cringed back fearfully but managed to keep hold of enough of her wits to find an answer. 'Well, I suppose nobody else noticed.'

'Blind are they?' sneered Dover. 'And bloody deaf, too?'

'Oh, Mr Tiffin made his exit most reverently. Well, you would expect that of him, wouldn't you? I would never have seen him myself if I hadn't been sitting right at the side of the church. Our old family pew, you know,' she explained proudly. 'I know Mr Liddle likes to have everybody sitting right in front of him so that he doesn't have to strain his voice but, as I told him, I have sat in that pew ever since I was a tiny child and I really don't see why ...'

Dover was no longer listening. He glared at MacGregor. 'Well?'

'But, wouldn't Mr Tiffin know that Miss Sampson could see him, sir?'

'I don't usually attend Evensong,' twittered Miss Sampson nervously. 'Not in the winter. It's the dark nights, you know.'

'Satisfied, now, moron?'

MacGregor shrugged his shoulders. 'I suppose so, sir.'

'There's no bloody suppose about it!' bellowed Dover. 'Tiffin knew to the minute what time Marsh would be on that path on his way to the station and he slipped out of the bloody church to kill him. We've got motive and opportunity. This old trout's fixed him.'

MacGregor sighed. 'Very good, sir. I'll go and get him.'

'And you stay there!' said Dover to Miss Sampson.

'Here?'

'Right there!' said Dover, starting off down the path towards the car. It was coming on to rain again and he'd no intention of catching his death for all the Arthur Tiffins in the world. 'You move an inch and I'll have you for obstructing the police in the execution of their duty and for attempting to withold vital evidence.'

'Oh, dear!' wailed Miss Sampson.

Dover hesitated. 'This stuff of yours any good for the bowels?' he asked.

Miss Sampson swayed. 'The ... ? Oh, no, I don't think so. I think you would require something quite different for ...'

'I'll risk it,' said Dover, coming back to relieve a trembling Miss Sampson of her burden. 'It might do some good though, with my constipation, I reckon it's a stick of dynamite ...'

MacGregor hurried off into the Tiffins' cottage and left Miss Sampson to Dover's tender mercies. The moving account of some of his difficulties had just reached a truly nauseating climax when it was interrupted by the arrival of a small, shabby car which came roaring up to the garden gate. The cub reporter from the local newspaper came tumbling out, terrified that he was going to miss the scoop of a lifetime.

'Is it true,' he panted, running up the garden path and catching Dover by the arm, 'that you're about to make an arrest in the murder of Gary Marsh?'

Dover fended him off. 'Who told you?'

The reporter dragged a fresh supply of air into his aching lungs. 'Lady Priscilla!' he gasped. 'She makes a point of tipping us off. Publicity for Beltour, you know.' He took another gulp. 'Have you caught the murderer?'

'I always get my man,' said Dover demurely.

The cub reporter dragged his notebook out. 'Can you give me a statement, chief inspector?'

Dover was just about to repel the young pup with a well chosen flea in his ear when the sheer beauty of the situation suddenly struck him. His face creased up and several stones of surplus fat began to wobble in a most alarming manner. The young reporter's mouth dropped open.

'I can't,' chuckled Dover as the tears spurted from his eyes and began to trickle down his podgy cheeks, 'give you any names at this stage but ...' – he broke off as the desire to laugh overcame him – 'but ... you can tell your readers ... it was the butler what done it!'

Available from Foul Play Press

Joyce Porter

American readers, having faced several lean years deprived of the company of Chief Inspector Wilfred Dover, will rejoice (so to speak) in the reappearance of "the most idle and avaricious policeman in the United Kingdom (and, possibly, the world)." Here is the series (in paperback) that introduced the bane of Scotland Yard and his hapless assistant, Sgt. MacGregor, to international acclaim.

Dover One	*192 pages*	*$ 5.95*
Dover Two	*222 pages*	*$ 5.95*
Dover Three	*192 pages*	*$ 4.95*
Dead Easy for Dover	*176 pages*	*$ 5.95*
Dover and the Unkindest Cut of All	*188 pages*	*$ 5.95*
Dover Goes to Pott	*192 pages*	*$ 5.95*
Dover Strikes Again	*202 pages*	*$ 5.95*
It's Murder With Dover	*192 pages*	*$ 5.95*

"Meet Detective Chief Inspector Wilfred Dover. He's fat, lazy, a scrounger and the worst detective at Scotland Yard. But you will love him."   —*Manchester Evening News*

Margot Arnold

The complete paperback adventures of Margot Arnold's beloved pair of peripatetic sleuths, Penny Spring and Sir Toby Glendower:

The Cape Cod Caper	*192 pages*	*$ 5.95*
Death of a Voodoo Doll	*220 pages*	*$ 5.95*
Death on the Dragon's Tongue	*224 pages*	*$ 4.95*
Exit Actors, Dying	*176 pages*	*$ 5.95*
Lament for a Lady Laird	*221 pages*	*$ 5.95*
The Menehune Murders	*272 pages*	*$ 5.95*
Toby's Folly	*256 pages*	*$ 5.95*
Zadock's Treasure	*192 pages*	*$ 5.95*

Available from bookstores, or by mail from the publisher: The Countryman Press, Box 175, Woodstock, VT 05091-0175. Please include $2.50 for shipping and handling. Write for a free Foul Play Press catalog.